The Me inside of Me

the me
inside of me

T. ERNESTO BETHANCOURT

Lerner Publications Company • Minneapolis

Manufactured in the United States of America

LIBRARY OF CONGRESS CATALOGING IN PUBLICATION DATA

Bethancourt, T. Ernesto.
  The me inside of me.

  Summary: When seventeen-year-old Alfredo Flores
suddenly becomes a very wealthy orphan, he discovers
having money creates a new set of unanticipated problems.
    [1. Mexican Americans—Fiction.   2. Wealth—Fiction]
I. Title.
PZ7.B46627Me 1985 [Fic] 85-10292
ISBN 0-8225-0728-5 (lib. bdg.)

  2 3 4 5 6 7 8 9 10 94 93 92 91 90 89 88 87 86

For Mel and Dolly Cebulash

I WAS IN BED WHEN THE NEWS CAME over the TV. I was also sick as a dog. I had a paper sack of used Kleenex next to my bed, and a night table full of pills, cough syrups, and various nose sprays close at hand. None of those things work, but they make you feel like you're doing something about being sick.

It was hot outside, the kind of hot you only find in Santa Amelia, California, in July. But because of my cold and the drafts from the air conditioner, I had the windows open and the conditioner shut off. Even when I don't have a cold, air conditioning gives me a stuffy nose. My mom always said that it runs in the family. We all have sinus trouble. I've had it since I was little.

I was watching "The Late Show" on TV. It was a "Rockford Files" rerun. I like James Garner. He's got the right balance between being *macho* and sensitive. It was one of those involved plots, with more turns than a merry-go-round. During the commercial breaks, I was working on a drawing that just wouldn't come out right.

Art is about my favorite course at Santa Amelia High. My teacher, Mr. Landesman, says I could maybe make a living off it someday. If I got the right training, that is. The drawing I was working on was of hands. Hands are my biggest hangup. No matter how hard I try, the way I draw hands seems just a little *off*. Not that they don't look like real hands; they do. They just don't look natural. It's hard to explain unless you could actually see what I was doing.

Mr. Landesman told me that if anything is tough, you've got to practice it. So I had laid out this drawing in black and white of nothing but arms and hands. They were all holding different things: hammers, wrenches, farm tools, and here and there a rifle. I was going to call the piece *Power to the People*. I once saw a mural like that in Mexico City and never forgot it. It was by Diego Rivera.

My picture wasn't coming out right. But I had plenty of time to work on it. And lots of peace and quiet, which is rare around our house. My whole family was on their way to Mexico City, and the house was empty except for me. I couldn't get on a plane all stuffed up the way I was. When you've got a heavy cold, the pressure inside the plane cabin has no place to go but your ears. And man, that is painful when it happens!

The reason my whole family—my mom, dad, and two sisters—were going to Mexico was a sad one. Outside of my immediate family, we only have one living relative, my grandfather's sister who lives in Mexico City. And she was dying of cancer. Her name is Matilda and she's the last member of our family that still lives in Mexico.

My grandfather came to Southern California fifty years ago. He was doing fine down in Mexico until the revolution, in the late 1920s. He had a law degree and was tied up heavy in politics. Trouble was, when the revolution came, he was on the losing side. If he'd have stayed in Mexico, he could have been shot, easy.

So, he came north to the States, where he worked as a gardener until he died. I know that sounds goofy. My *abuelo* was an educated man with a law degree. But all he was in California was a gardener. Law is one of those things you can spend a lifetime learning. But when you go to another country, you don't know diddly-squat. If it comes to that, even a lawyer from a different state inside the USA can have a hard time passing the exams for California.

And when Abuelo came to this country, he was

already close to thirty years old. Losing all he had in Mexico seemed to snap something inside him. He didn't ever learn any English outside of enough to get along. It was like he didn't care anymore. The same Wilfredo Flores, who had been a big-deal lawyer in Mexico, never ran anything but a lawnmower in the States.

Anyhow, his sister Matilda was now dying. My dad always had the idea that Aunt Tilda was rich. At least she always found the coins to send for the family once a year. The idea was that us kids, although we're all born here, same as my dad, should never forget where we originally came from.

With Aunt Tilda dying, the whole family was supposed to go down to Mexico City and sit by her bedside. I guess my dad figured when the old girl cashed in her chips, she was going to leave a bundle to the Flores family in Santa Amelia. But being so sick, I couldn't make the flight. I wrote a letter to Aunt Tilda in Spanish. My dad had me do it. Oh, I would have done it anyhow, but the old man wanted the letter to have the right tone. He had to check it out. My Spanish is for the birds.

I checked the clock at my bedside. It was almost twelve-thirty. I suddenly remembered that I hadn't phoned Mrs. Fernandez. She's my mom's friend up the block from where we live. I promised I'd do that. It's funny. I'm almost eighteen years old, but my mom couldn't go off anywhere without leaving me with some sort of babysitter. Must be force of habit. Because of my two younger sisters, Mom got used to having a sitter in the house when she was away. She had to ask Mrs. Fernandez to look in on me.

I was wondering if I should telephone when it was so late. We live in an area in Santa Amelia that's mostly working people who get up early. My dad worked at a plastics factory. He was a machine mechanic. He fixed whatever went wrong with the molding equipment. It's a good trade, and our little house is almost paid off.

Not that the Flores family was rich. But we weren't living in any *barrio*, either. True, all the families around us are Chicano, but the neighborhood is all one-family houses, well kept. The streets are clean and we don't have too many ripoffs.

I was just deciding whether to call Mrs. Fernandez when the news came on. It wasn't supposed to be on. "The Late Show" goes to part two without a news break. Usually the part two is a "Columbo" or a "Hart to Hart" rerun. So when "Rockford" ended, I was ready to switch off the lights and sack out. But tonight was different. The Japanese lady newscaster they have on the regular news came on camera and said:

"We interrupt our regular programming to bring you a news bulletin. A West Coastal airliner, bound for Mexico City from Los Angeles, has crashed just north of the Mexico City airport. Eyewitnesses report that flames from the wreckage were visible

11

for a mile. No further details as to survivors are available at this time. We will bring you further news as it develops. We now return to our regular programming."

I felt a lead weight in the pit of my stomach. The flight she was talking about *had* to be the one my family was on! It's the late flight, and the cheapest one, to Mexico City. The Chicanos call it the cattle flight. That's on account of years ago, a lot of Mexicans used to sneak into this country on railroad cars with cattle in them. Or maybe the other way around. In empty cattle cars coming back. But one thing I knew for sure. It's the only flight on West Coastal to Mexico City at that hour.

I was about to pick up the phone and call the airport, when it rang. I jumped. You know how sometimes when you're about to call, and your hand is just a fraction of an inch from the phone receiver and it rings? It scares you. And I was already worked up.

"This is Mr. Hansen, of West Coastal Airlines," said the voice. "To whom am I speaking?"

"This is Fred Flores," I replied.

"Are you related to Jose, Irene, Lorene and Esp... uh, Esper..."

I could hear that the *gringo* was having trouble pronouncing my sister's name: Esperanza. And the lump in my stomach jumped all the way up to my throat. I knew very well what was coming, but I didn't want to believe it.

"Are you trying to say Esperanza?" I asked.

"Yes, yes. That's it. Are you any relation to these people?"

"Yeah," I said. "They're my family. All of them. What's going on?"

"It's my sad duty to tell you, Mr. Flores, that our Flight 245 to Mexico City, with the people named aboard, has fallen just outside the Mexico City airport. There were no survivors. Now there are certain details which we must go into, to confirm identification. I realize that this is shocking news and..."

The *gringo's* voice kept going, but I didn't hear any more. I was hoping against hope that he'd say somebody in my family was still alive. Even when you know in your heart that it's the worst news in the world, you keep on hoping. I hung up the phone while the guy from the airline was still talking. Why not? I'd heard all he had to say that mattered to me.

The room got a little blurry about then. I guess it was tears. I got out of bed and walked into the kitchen. This may sound goofy, but I didn't tear my hair or scream or anything like that. I went to the Frigidaire and got myself a glass of milk. There was a Van de Kamps coffee cake on the workboard near the sink. I cut myself a piece of cake and sat down at the table.

I couldn't choke down a bite or take a swallow of milk. In fact, I don't know why I did such a thing. Since then, I read in books how when a tragedy hits you, the first thing you do is something normal. You try to convince yourself that it hasn't really happened. I guess that's why I set out the cake and milk.

After looking at the cake and milk for a few minutes, I got up from the table. I walked down the hall from the kitchen to where my sisters, Lorene and Esperanza, shared a room. I turned on the light in my sisters' room and looked inside. It wasn't any different from before I knew they were dead. The room was waiting for Esperanza and Lorene to come home. All Lorene's Snoopy dolls were where they were supposed to be. The big poster of Erik Estrada on the wall was still smiling down at Esperanza's bed. Their stereo set was where it should have been. But they weren't coming back to this room. Ever.

Finally, I went into my folks' bedroom. I looked at the crucifix over the bed, the wedding picture of Mom and Dad on the wall, and the pictures of all us kids on the dresser. The room started getting blurry again. As I stood in the middle of the room, the reality hit me fully for the first time.

I let out a holler. It was a cry of hurt and pain. It came from somewhere deep inside me and it hurt my throat when it came out. I fell down across my parents' big double bed and I began screaming into the mattress, so no one could hear: "Mama! Papa!" I cried until I fell asleep.

14

WHEN THE SUN CAME UP, I WAS STILL
lying there, across my parents' bed. For a crazy
minute, I didn't know where I was. I never slept
in there. Then it all came rushing back. I was
alone in the house. And I always would be.

I got up, went to the john and went through the
whole routine anyone does each morning. It all
seemed so pointless. And crazily, through it all, I
kept telling myself that my folks would be phoning
any minute now. But each time I tried to tell myself
they were only away on a long weekend in Mexico
City, the truth kept coming out of the dark corners
of my mind. Like a toothache that you take a
painkiller for. It doesn't hurt as sharply as it did

before you took the medicine, but you know it's still there, ready to hurt again, once the painkiller wears off.

There was the beginning of the day, shiny bright and already hot. I could hear cars and trucks passing by, a few blocks away. We live on a side street, but in the mornings, you can hear the traffic. Especially in summertime when the sound carries.

I looked at myself as I brushed my teeth. I was just like the house. You couldn't tell from looking at me that I was empty inside. I had no more tears to cry. I left the last of them on the pillows of my parents' bed.

I showed my teeth to myself in the mirror. It might have looked like a smile, but it wasn't. It was just the way you do that, after brushing your teeth. I thought a shower might help, and took a long, hot one. It's more cooling on a hot day. It didn't help my frame of mind, but I figured I could cope better if I got out of pajamas and dressed.

When I went into the empty kitchen, the glass of milk and piece of coffee cake were where I'd left them the night before. I spilled the milk into the sink and chucked the piece of cake in the trash. It hit the bottom of the can with a hollow thump. From being out on the table all night, it was hard as a rock.

The house was silent, as only an empty house can be. I felt like a ghost wandering around a graveyard. The Frigidaire cut on, and the motor sounded loud. I could hear all sorts of things in the emptiness. The little creaks and groans the roof timbers made as they heated up in the July sun that beat down on the shingles. The faint hum of the electric kitchen clock that hung over the stove. I nearly jumped out of my skin when the phone rang.

"Hullo?" I said.

"Good morning," said a cheery woman's voice. "This is Nannette Wilson, I'm with West Coastal Airlines. Our representative, Mr. Hansen, called last night. Is this Mr. Flores?"

I almost said, "No, this is Freddie. Mr. Flores is in Mexico City." See, all my life, I've been Freddie and my dad has been Mr. Flores. But I realized what this woman from the airline meant. And in that same moment, I realized that from now on, I *was* Mr. Flores. There wasn't any other. Or was there? A crazy hope sprang up inside me.

"Yes, this is Mr. Flores," I said. "Is there some news about my parents and sisters?"

There was a brief silence on the line. Then the woman's voice said, "No, sir. I was calling to set up an appointment with you. Didn't Mr. Hansen er... inform you of..."

"He told me that all my family were killed."

"Well, that is correct, Mr. Flores," she said. "But in order to be certain..."

"You mean some of the passengers are still alive?" I shouted.

17

"No, no. I'm deeply sorry, Mr. Flores. There were no survivors on Flight 245. It's a question of identification of the deceased. We must have some sort of confirmation. If you would be able to..."

I hung up the phone. What a bunch of ghouls! I get a call in the middle of the night, telling me this airline has killed my entire family. Then the next day, like they were ordering coffee and sweet rolls for breakfast, they want me to come and identify the bodies!

The phone rang again.

I grabbed it off the hook, ready to really give that airline woman an earful. But it wasn't her calling. It was long distance from Mexico. I went through the drill of identifying myself in English, then Spanish.

From a distance came the voice of my Aunt Tilda. "Alfredito, is that you?" she said in Spanish. "A terrible thing has happened."

"*Sí*, yes, I know, Auntie," I said. "It was on TV. And the airline called."

"Ay, *Dios*, what a tragedy!" she said, and started to cry. "To think that they were coming here to say goodbye to an old woman. Now they are dead. All of them! Ay, Alfredito! I can't stand it!"

I spent a few minutes saying a bunch of things I didn't believe. Stuff like: "It's God's will. We don't understand why it happened, but it's all for the best."

All the time I was thinking, why is it God's will? What kind of God kills kids like my sisters? What

18

had they ever done to die, before they even got a chance to live? Collect stuffed animals, and pictures of rock stars they'd never meet?

Every Sunday, when I was a kid, I went to mass with my folks. I think I understood about Jesus. He was that man, there on the cross, with nails in his hands, and a crown of thorns. He did his best to teach everyone about love. But the world wasn't ready for what he had to say. They killed him.

Then, there was this other person: God. He was the one who let Jesus die. He was the one who let my whole family die. Why? What did they ever do that was so bad?

I didn't believe all the things I said to Aunt Tilda. But I knew they were things she wanted to hear. She's an old, sick woman. She only leaves her house to get chemotherapy and go to church. The treatments aren't working. If she gets comfort from the church, who am I to throw stones?

I realized I was just running on. I suddenly didn't want to talk any more. I cut in on her, before she could start up again on church talk.

"The airline wants me to go down there and identify the . . . family," I said. I couldn't bring myself to say *bodies*.

"There's no need," my aunt said tearfully. "I have just come from the *deposito*, the morgue. It is true, Alfredito. They are gone. All of them!" Then she started crying again. And I started consoling her again.

19

It's an odd thing. The fact that my aunt was falling to pieces somehow made me stronger. I talked with her for another fifteen minutes. She had hired a lawyer down there to handle all the details. She was asking me if it was okay to bury my family in Mexico. Or did I want to have the remains shipped back to Santa Amelia for burial?

"I guess I'd want them up here," I said. "I'd like a last look."

"But there is no one to see!" she wailed. "The plane burned when it fell. The authorities could only use the passenger list to identify the dead. Alfredito, you will be shipping just boxes of ashes to *los Estados Unidos*. We have the family plot here. Your *abuelo* was buried here."

"I know, I know," I said. I remembered how it was Abuelo's last wish to be buried there. And how we shipped his coffin to Mexico. "But they belong here, with me," I said.

"Please, 'Fredo," she said. "Let them stay here. Soon, I will be joining them. I have lived with death for the past two years. Once a month, I visit the grave of my husband and my brother. I will see that your dear ones get a proper ceremony."

"But I'll be coming down," I protested.

"You are a child, 'Fredo," she said. "You know nothing of such things. I, God help me, have buried all of my family."

"I don't know, Auntie," I said. "This is all happening so fast..."

"*Precísamente,*" Aunt Tilda said. "Allow me to handle the details. I know how, I weep to say. I have already spoken with your *abuleo's* friend, Callen the lawyer in Santa Amelia. He will have the ticket for you to come to Mexico City."

"Now wait a second," I began. I was beginning to feel like I was a puppet, with Auntie pulling the strings.

"My poor Alfredito," she soothed. "This is a terrible time. You are not thinking clearly. Allow an old woman her foolishness, if that is what you think it to be. I have done this before. And also, you are too young to sign the necessary papers."

She was right there. I wouldn't be eighteen for another ten months. And all that lets you do is vote in a federal election. For the rest of your rights, you're a kid until you're twenty-one.

"Then why bother to ask me?" I said. "You're running it anyway." I was starting to get mad.

"Don't act this way, 'Fredo," she pleaded. "Just call Señor Callen. Do you have the number?"

"Yeah. It's in Dad's address book, in the kitchen."

"*Bueno,*" she said. "Now, I must be doing things. And this call is costing a fortune. I will expect you whenever Señor Callen makes the arrangements." Before I could say anything more, she had hung up.

I replaced the phone on the kitchen wall hook and sat down at the table. I knew I should eat something. My nose was all blocked up again from my cold and the constant feeling that I was going

21

to break down and cry some more. I could feel a far-off wave of nausea begin in my empty stomach. I managed to choke down a glass of milk with Instant Breakfast in it. Then, with a rush, it came up. I couldn't make it down the hall to the bathroom in time. I knew that. I got over to the kitchen sink and tossed.

All the time I was retching into the sink, I kept thinking: Gee, Mom will be sore at me for messing up the kitchen. Then, after my stomach spasms subsided and I had wiped my face with a paper towel from the holder over the sink, it came back to me. There was nobody going to be sore at me. Ever again.

I went back to the john and brushed the sour taste out of my mouth with Gleem, and then I went to my bedroom. I sat down on the bed and looked at the drawing I had been working on during the night. It didn't look like anything. I picked it up and tore it across the middle.

The phone rang. I let it ring; I didn't want to talk to anyone. I sat on my bed for most of the day. About four-thirty that afternoon, I called the lawyer.

"IT'S BEEN EIGHT WEEKS, FREDDIE,"
Callen said to me. "You have to snap out of it.
Life goes on. Plans must be made."

"Swell," I said flatly. I was in the law offices of
John J. Callen, in Santa Amelia. It was in one of
the older buildings in the downtown area. There was
a time when the area was considered choice. Now,
it's mostly pawn shops, cut-rate stores and cheap
bars. But Callen has been practicing law in Santa
Amelia for over fifty years. He was one of the first
tenants in the rundown old office building, and he's
stayed there ever since.

But that's not how he got to be a friend of my
grandfather's. Abuelo was his gardener for many

years. And when the neighborhood around the downtown area began to change, Callen began getting more and more Chicano clients. At the time, Callen didn't speak any Spanish. But he knew from talking with my grandfather that Abuelo had once been a lawyer in Mexico.

Over the years, Abuelo was a translator of documents and interpreter for Callen. Until Callen hired a young Chicano law student to work in the office. He had offered my grandfather the job, but Abuelo had turned it down. Like I say, the old man had lost all heart for law. He said it was too close to what he'd been trained for. But by law, he wasn't allowed to do it for a living in the States.

And he wouldn't take any money for what he did for Callen, either. It was because Callen treated Abuelo like an equal; a fellow professional. And always called him Mister Flores, or *abogado*, when clients were around. Abuelo always called Callen Jack in private and Callen called Abuelo Wilfredo. Never Willie, the way his gardening customers did.

So what Callen did for Abuelo in return was to give special presents to Abuelo's children and grandchildren on their birthdays and holidays. The first wristwatch I ever had, I got from Señor Callen on my tenth birthday. Callen was like an extra grandfather to me.

Not that we saw a lot of him. We didn't. He stayed in his part of town with all the other rich Anglos, and we lived where we did. After all, as

Abuelo explained, Callen was a business friend of his. But Abuelo was a very formal man. Most educated Latinos of his generation are. Or were, I should say. I realized that Callen had asked me a question. I'd been inside myself and not listening.

"I'm sorry, Mr. Callen. What were you saying."

"I was saying that you must think of your future, Freddie," he said. "The court has appointed me your guardian, with your Aunt Matilda's approval. It saves settlements under international law. And as your parents were native-born Americans..."

"That's a laugh," I snorted. "All their lives, they got called Mexicans. They had to die to become native-born Americans, huh?"

"I won't go into that," said Callen cooly. "We are here to discuss your future, Freddie. As it happens, you are a rather wealthy young man now."

"Yeah, I know," I said.

See, Mom had this thing about flying. Every time she'd get on a plane, she was sure it was going to fall. So before she'd get on a flight, she always used to pump lots of coins into those insurance machines they have at the airport. For once, she was right. Because I was the only one who wasn't flying on the plane that fell, she had taken out policies on everyone. Right up to the maximum amount, with me getting it all.

What a rotten joke. My old man would have to work a million years to make what he was worth dead. The whole thing stunk, so far as I was con-

25

cerned. Sure, I knew I was worth easy a quarter of a million bucks on insurance alone.

Then, too, Callen had brought a lawsuit against West Coastal Airlines for fifteen million dollars. He already told me that chances were I'd see a million five on the settlement. More, if I waited until it came to trial. Outside of Callen sticking it to West Coastal for killing my whole family, I didn't care about that, either.

When it came right down to it, I didn't care much about anything. Ever since that night, I couldn't. I didn't have any tears left, either.

My Aunt Tilda had commented on how brave I was, and how grownup, when I stood at the graveside in Mexico dry-eyed. She didn't know. I was all hollowed out inside. I just plain didn't care anymore. I was going through the motions. After all, like she herself had said, all we were burying was boxes of ashes. I had done my crying four days before the funeral and two thousand miles away.

"How have you been getting along? At home, I mean?" asked Callen. "Are you eating regularly? You look a bit thin."

"I'm getting along just fine," I told him. "My mom's friend from down the block, Mrs. Hernandez ...she takes care of the house. She even stays longer than she needs to, because she gets to watch the shows she likes on our TV. At her daughter's house, she can't. At first a lot of people from church were bringing food over to me. But now, mostly

I've been eating out. Don't worry about me."

"But that's part of my job now," Callen said. "I worry. You'll be my concern for the next few years, Freddie. And if I can be of help, or offer guidance, that's what I'm here for."

"Thanks, I appreciate that," I said. "I'll keep it in mind."

Callen looked at me sharply. He hadn't missed my tone of voice. I didn't care. But Callen wasn't ready to quit.

"Have you given any thought to your schooling, Freddie?" he asked. "It's almost the first week in September."

"What's to think about?" I said dully. "The school is two blocks away. I graduate next June. So what?"

"Dammit boy!" said Callen hitting his desktop with the flat of his hand. "Mooning about the past won't bring your family back. I thought of your father as almost a son. And you could easily be my grandson. The court has placed me in charge of your life for the next three years. But how can I help you if all you want to do is brood?"

"Where does your grandson go to school?" I asked.

I watched Callen shift in his chair over that question. He's a very pink man. His hair is pure white and thin and the scalp shines through bright pink. He's in his seventies and shaped like a large pink oval. He's one of the whiter white men I know. My question about his grandson was more like a cheap shot than a real inquiry. It wouldn't be likely that I'd ever go any place John J. Callen's grandson went. Not unless I was waiting tables.

"Well, my grandson is a bit older than you are, Freddie," he hedged. "He's already in college."

"But where does he go?" I pressed.

"Stanford," Callen said. "But as I say, he's older than you are. You still have a year of high school to finish. And then too, I don't know what preparation you have for a higher education, what courses you've taken."

"I'm in the top twenty in my class," I said quickly. I wasn't going to let him off the hook. "My grades run from B-plus to A's."

"Very good!" said Callen smiling. "You should have no trouble enrolling in any of the colleges in our area. There are many fine schools. When you're about ready to begin the second half of your senior year, we'll look over the colleges together."

"I want Stanford," I said. Now, this just wasn't so. I couldn't have cared less. What had set me off was Callen telling me about my "native-born American" parents and how I could be his grandson. What a crock! I don't know who he thought he was jiving, but I wanted him to know he wasn't blowing smoke in this kid's eyes. But before I knew it, I had gone too far to stop.

"There are rigid scholastic requirements for Stanford, Freddie," he said to me. "And although Santa Amelia High is an excellent school, there may be some courses you haven't taken. You may have to alter your curriculum, if there's time, before you apply for Stanford."

"You mean if I'm smart enough to be an 'A' student in Santa Amelia, I'm not good enough to go to Stanford?" I said. "Or is it a different kind of smart we're talking about?"

I could see I'd gotten to him. Callen is pink, but far from dumb. He knew exactly what I was driving at. I was waiting for him to come up with a bunch of reasons why a Mexican kid, with an ordinary city school education, couldn't get inside the holy gates of Stanford. I have to admit that I misjudged Callen.

"No, we're not talking about a different kind of smart," he said. "But if you think you can slip me the needle because I'm a *gringo*, let me tell you some rather nasty truths, young man."

He got up from his desk and started walking back and forth, like he was in front of a judge and jury, pleading a case.

"To begin with, Freddie, you go to a school in a Spanish ghetto area. Scholastic standards *should* be as high as elsewhere. But frankly, they are not. When teachers are concerned for their personal safety and mostly come from non-Latin backgrounds, they don't understand the students. They fear them, when they don't hold them in contempt." He stopped when he saw the look on my face.

"Oh, you're surprised I know this?" he said. "Why shouldn't I know it? I've been representing Latinos in Santa Amelia for years. I know good and well that there are two kinds of law enforcement. One for the middle-class Anglos, and another for Latinos.

"In the same way, the education you got was not equal to other more wealthy school districts. It's the truth. It's nasty, but God help us, it's the truth. No, I don't think that even with straight A's you could pass the requirements for any topflight school. There's no reflection on your intelligence, nor your race. It's a sad commentary on local politics."

I sat there like he'd all of a sudden started to speak in Spanish. Sure, I'd heard these words before. But never from an Anglo!

"If you know all this, how come you let it happen?" I asked.

"*I* let it happen?" mocked Callen. "How much power do you think I have? And quite frankly, the Latino population lets it happen, too. They have votes. They don't demand what they are entitled to by law."

"They don't know what to ask for," I said.

"That is most definitely not *my* responsibility," Callen said. "I am a professional man, not a crusader. Yes, I see to it that any client of mine gets his fair shake from the judicial system. But past that, I have had my own family to raise, my own career to follow. I started broke, and made what I have by my own efforts. So kindly don't give me that baloney about why didn't *I* do something. As Ben Franklin said: 'The Lord helps those who help themselves'!"

"All right," I said. "I'm helping myself. I got the money to go to Stanford. I can go anywhere. I don't even have to work, if I don't want to. I could drop out and do nothing for the rest of my life." I let it sink in on Callen. "But I want to go to Stanford. You say what I got for an education isn't good enough. How do I go, just the same?"

Callen scratched his chin, thinking. Then he went behind his desk again and got out a notebook. He pushed a button on his desk intercom and when his secretary answered he said, "Mrs. Cooper, get me Allen Schuler at Valverde Academy. You should have the number there." In a few minutes, the intercom buzzed and Callen picked up the phone.

"Hullo, Allen! Good to hear from you, too. Say listen. I have this young man who has just become my ward. Yes, orphaned. He's pulling good grades in his junior year in high school... what school? Santa Amelia High... Flores, Freddie Flores... yes, he is." Callen looked over his desk at me and gave me a huge wink. I knew that this Schuler guy had just asked if I was a Chicano.

Callen continued his conversation: "Did you read about the West Coastal flight that fell in Mexico this July?... Yes, that's the one. Well, this boy is the only surviving member of his family... yes, it sure is a tough one. Anyway, he wants to go to Stanford next year. Can you have him ready by then?... I see. All right, that's what we'll do. Meet you for lunch, say... twelve-thirty will be fine. Yes, you too, Allen." Callen hung up and returned his attention to me.

"Freddie," he said, "have you ever heard of Valverde Academy?"

"Nope."

"It's a prep school, on the Palos Verdes peninsula," Callen said. "They specialize in getting young people into good colleges. It's a coeducational school, and the students live on campus. It runs year-round. And I want you to know that it's incredibly tough, scholastically. They don't waste time with niceties at Valverde. If you don't do the work well, they'll chuck you straight out, understand?"

"Sounds like a jail," I said.

"Hardly a jail, Freddie. Valverde has the highest rate of graduates accepted by major colleges of any prep school in this part of the country. They are proud of their reputation, and any student who looks like he might mess up that reputation is weeded out early on. Their enrollment is predicated on the results they get."

"You're saying that if they don't deliver the goods, they go out of business?" I asked.

"As good a way of putting it as any, Freddie."

"Then it's fine with me," I said. "I'll go there."

"Hold your horses, young man," Callen said. "You first have to pass their basic requirements to enroll. Schuler needs a transcript of your high school records."

"He can get it easy," I said. "And I wasn't jiving.

My marks are great. The only thing I got trouble with is math. That's my one weak spot. Well, maybe my English grammar and punctuation could be better," I admitted.

"Then you should have no trouble. Only I have the trouble now."

"How come?"

"Because I have to have lunch with Allen Schuler," smiled Callen. "And he's the deadliest bore in this county."

We both laughed. Then Callen said, "But granted Valverde accepts you, there will be the problem of your parents' house."

"What kind of problem?"

"You'll be living at the Academy," Callen explained. "The house will be empty. Perhaps we can sell the house..."

"No way!" I said quickly. "That's my house. I grew up in that house."

"Make sense, Freddie. You won't be using the place. You know that it will be broken into if you leave it untended. If you are that attached to the place, you could rent it out..."

"No! I won't do that!" I said. "I don't want anything in that house touched. I want it just the way it is. I won't have strangers in it!"

Callen sighed heavily. "Freddie, Freddie. If it's vacant, it will be robbed. If it's rented, you'd have to get your possessions out of it anyway. Now, do you really want to go to Valverde or not? Their

33

rules are quite specific. You live on campus. It's got to be one way or another."

"Who says?" I came back. I had an idea. "Mrs. Fernandez up the block. She lives with her married daughter. I know she'd live in the place and take care of it for me. In fact, she wouldn't touch anything in my folks' or sisters' rooms. That's the way I want it: nothing moved or touched."

"That's a very sensitive and thoughtful gesture, Freddie," Callen said. "But also an expensive one. You're losing money by not renting or selling. And you have to learn about managing money. You'll have a great deal of it when you turn twenty-one."

"Okay with me," I said. "I been all my life without money. Now I got more than I could ever spend. If I'm going to be as rich as you say, I can afford it."

"As you wish, Freddie. Are you sure Mrs. Fernandez will do this?"

"*Seguro*," I said. "She sleeps on a convertible sofa at her daughter's house. She can have my room all to herself."

"Very well, Freddie," Callen said. "I'll trust you to get Mrs. Fernandez over here to sign an agreement. Which reminds me, how are you getting around?"

"Dad left the keys to the Olds, in case of an emergency," I explained. "I've got my license. I've been using the family car."

"Is that the same Olds I've been seeing for the past few years?"

34

"That's it. It's a '69."

"Well, you'll need a more dependable car," Callen said. "I have some connections in the business community. We should see about getting you your own car, and some wardrobe for school."

I thought about what I was wearing: jeans, sneakers, and a tee shirt. "You mean I got to clean up to go to Valverde, is that it?"

"Oh Freddie, you're so thin-skinned," Callen said sadly. "This is a school attended by the richest kids in our area. It's not the sort of school where one wears...well, what you are wearing now. And you certainly wouldn't drive an old junker car."

"A bunch of snobs, huh?"

"If you want to think of it that way," Callen said, his face set. "Or, if you prefer, you can think of it this way: You are a rich young man. It's quite acceptable for you to dress well and to drive a good, new car. You wouldn't go to a dance at your high school dressed the way you are now, would you?"

"Of course not," I admitted. "I'd dress up."

"Then you understand what I'm getting at," Callen said. He opened his middle desk drawer and came up with a business card. He handed it to me. "This is a friend of mine who owns a Chevrolet agency. I'll telephone to let him know you'll be coming in. You pick out a new car."

"I'll go right to this dealer from here," I said. "God knows, I don't have anyone waiting for me at home."

"And don't forget clothes for school, Freddie,"

Callen added. "Clothes are the first impression you make. How are you fixed for cash? Do you still have anything left of the money I advanced to you?"

About a month before, Callen had given me a couple of hundred bucks. He was already paying all the bills at my folks' house. It was just "walking around money," he'd said.

"Sure, I replied. "I've got almost all of it."

"Very good!" smiled Callen. "You've a good sound head on your shoulders, Freddie."

"Thanks," I said.

But I didn't explain why I had almost all the coins. See, I wasn't going anywhere or doing anything. I didn't have the heart. Ever since that night when the plane crashed, I hadn't cared about much. When you stay inside the house and watch TV, you don't spend anything. And I don't smoke, drink, or dope. And there was more to it than that.

When the word got out in my neighborhood about my folks, everyone was super kind, at first. Any place I went, somebody would come up to me and say how sorry they were about my family. I never knew so many people knew me. Then, the other business started up.

I began to get stuff in the mail. Before my family died, I think I maybe got a half-dozen letters in my whole life. But when the news hit the papers, about all the money I was supposed to have, I got MAIL. Almost everyone in the world wanted to advise me on what to do with my new fortune:

stocks, bonds, weird inventions. After I read the first fifty letters or so, I didn't bother opening up any more.

Then there were my "cousins." Anybody whose last name was Flores wrote to me, asking for money. That's a laugh, right there. Flores is one of the most common Latino names there is. Like, if your name was Smith. and you heard about another Smith who was rich, would you write, asking him for money? It seemed that every time I turned around, someone wanted a piece of me or my supposed millions. Maybe I should have expected it.

But what I didn't expect was the way my old friends starting acting. Ray Prieto and Artie Lopez have been my pals all my life. We've been through a few scrapes, a couple of fights, and lots of years together. These were guys who knew me as plain old Freddie Flores.

We were at the drive-in, having the usual burgers and stuff. Then, when the waitress brought us the bill, neither Ray nor Artie made a move to even look at it. I picked it up and added up what I'd had, like always. I put my money on the table.

"That's for my end," I said.

"Come on, Freddie," Ray said. "What are you, chintzy or something?"

"What are you talking about?" I asked.

"Don't kid us," Artie said. "You got millions. I read it in the paper. It said your lawyer's suing the airline for fifteen million bucks!"

"That's nothing to me," I said. "So far, I ain't seen dime one. I got what I got. Now, are you guys gonna pay your end of this tab, or not?"

I don't know why I said it. It really didn't make any difference to me. Maybe it was all the mail I'd got, trying to squeeze a buck out of me. Maybe it was all my phony "cousins." I never expected this from Ray and Artie. And Artie was genuinely ticked off!

"You see how tight people get when they get a few bucks?" he said to Ray. "I'll see you around, high roller," he said to me. Then he actually got up and walked away from the table. He stopped at the door and turned. "You coming, Ray?" he asked.

Ray gave me a sheepish grin and stood up. "I gotta go, Freddie," he said. He fished in his pocket for some money.

"Don't bother," I said. "I got it covered."

"You don't have to, Freddie," he said.

"Oh, don't I?" I came back. "It looks like even my friends have a price tag on them, lately."

Ray's face fell. He walked off without another word. I felt like a rat. But I wasn't about to admit how much Artie's words had hurt me.

I saw Artie and Ray a few times after that, but it was never the same. I didn't feel any different, but to them, I was all of a sudden another person. My old pals never came by or called. And I sure wasn't going to call them. I started staying in the house more and more. The money I hadn't even seen was already costing me my friends.

I told all this to Callen. He sat back, and laughed real hard. "Well, that's your first lesson in handling money, Freddie," he said. "You did the right thing, by the way. Just because you have money doesn't mean you're compelled to be foolish with it."

"It wasn't that," I replied quickly. "Not the coin. It was like I was a different person to Ray and Artie. I mean, I just think of me as me. If I got money, that's fine. But I'm still *me*. Don't you see?"

"Indeed, I do," Callen smiled. "But to Artie and Ray, you *are* somebody different now. You have money, and lots of it. If you examine the matter, you'll see it too. You recall how in your neighborhood, the people with money are always *they* and *them*?"

"Sure."

"Well, Freddie, you have just become one of *them*," Callen explained. "And you can never go back. There will always be that distance between you and your old friends. The money has changed it all."

"But, I'm the same Freddie Flores," I protested. "I just have some money. Money I never asked for. And the way I got it, I'd give every cent to have my family back."

"You ought to read F. Scott Fitzgerald, Freddie," smiled Callen. "He had an excellent grasp of how money separates people from each other."

"*The very rich are different from you and me,*" I quoted, and saw Callen's eyebrows shoot up. "Don't be so surprised," I said. "I read all of Fitzgerald's books. They got those things out in comic book form," I added nastily.

Callen roared with laughter. "You *are* your grandfather's grandson, aren't you?" he said. "That's the kind of answer I'd have expected from Wilfredo. There's much of the stiff-necked Spanish pride in you, son."

"I come by it honestly," I said.

"You surely do," Callen admitted. "I admired your grandpa a great deal, Freddie. He was a rare man. But the system broke him, boy. He gave up the fight. All he did at my office was relive the days in Mexico when he was a figure of respect. But it was pretending, don't you see? Once he left this office, he was Willie the gardener again. I don't think many understood that."

"I always did," I said. "Me and Abuelo were tight. My Spanish isn't too good, but we used to talk, sometimes. Yeah, he lived in the past. You're right."

"Well then," Callen said, scoring his point, "I know that you won't make the same mistake. Your old friends, your old house: they're all part of the past. You can't live in it, and you can't go backwards in time. You're changed. The money has changed you, whether you admit it or not."

"Maybe you're right," I said, grudgingly.

"No maybe about it. I am right," Callen said firmly. "And now, young man, I do have other clients.

You have the agency card to go get your car. And don't let Andy Grober screw you on your trade-in, either. He owns the agency, and he owes me. I'll have Mrs. Cooper draw you a check for another five hundred dollars. You go out shopping today. Buy some new clothes for school. Get yourself a car. And Freddie?"

"Yeah?"

"Don't live in the past. You've a brilliant future before you, if you can seize the opportunity. My door is always open to you. You're sort of my son now." He stuck out his hand for a handshake.

I took Callen's hand, realizing that it was the first time I had ever shaken his hand. Come to think of it, I never saw Callen shake hands with my father, either. Just Abuelo.

I got up and went to the door, then stopped. "I want you to know that I appreciate what you're doing, Mr. Callen. I mean the school and all."

"Nonsense, boy!" smiled Callen. "It's your money you're spending. Make sure you get your money's worth, that's all!"

I left the office and went off to buy a new car.

IT WAS A BRIGHT CANARY-YELLOW Corvette, with red and black racing stripes. The interior was red, and it had every extra you could name. The big engine, a four-on-the-floor, AM/FM stereo with a tape player and buttons to push the buttons. I could just see myself driving into Lara's Drive-In and watching the looks on the faces. I wanted to sit inside it and tried the door. It was locked.

"What are you doing there?" said a voice from behind me. I looked around and saw this big Anglo dude with a red face, white shirt, polyester slacks, and a name tag on his shirt pocket that read "George."

"I wanted to sit in the car," I explained.

"The car is locked," George said.

"I can see that," I came back. "Can you open it?"

"Yes, I can," George says, real snotty. "Are you going to buy it?"

Right away, I knew what was going down. Old George here sees this Chicano kid on the showroom floor, trying to open the door to a real expensive car. He probably figures I want to cop an ashtray or the cigarette lighter. Or maybe he figures I'm going to contaminate this swell car with my greasy Chicano hands.

I thought about what Callen and I discussed at the office. How I shouldn't act like I'm a poor kid because I'm not anymore. Maybe I was acting snotty when I did what I did then. I should have shown this guy the card Callen gave me.

But that isn't what I wanted. See, I give this dude the card, right away, it's all right. But only because a big lawyer like Callen says it's okay. Not because Alfredo Flores has the coins; just because another Anglo says I'm okay. I didn't want it that way. So when George asks me am I going to buy this car, I say, "I was thinking about it. But I'm not buying any car I don't test drive first. And I'm sure not buying a car I can't so much as sit in."

"Listen kid," George says, getting even redder in the face, "that's an expensive car. I saw the junker you drove up in. If you're in the market for a car, there are lots of used cars on the outside. I sell

43

new cars, and I'm not wasting my time demonstrating something you'll never buy. Or hope to buy. My time is worth money. And kid, you're not worth my time."

I gave old George an evil grin and said, "Tell me, George. How much commission would you make on this car, if I bought it? A few hundred bucks, maybe?" I reached into my pocket. I'd been by the bank and cashed the check Callen gave me for five hundred dollars. I got it all in hundreds. I guess because I never saw a hundred-dollar bill before. I flashed the money under George's nose.

"Look at this, George," I said. I took one of the hundreds and held it up. Then carefully, I tore it in half lengthwise. I put the two halves together and tore them again. I tore the quarters in half, watching old George's face with each tear. When I was done, I threw the pieces up in the air and let them come fluttering down.

"Confetti," I said, grinning real nasty. Then I reached into my tee shirt pocket and took out the business card Callen had given to me. I handed it to George. "Now George," I said, "you go get Mr. Grober. You tell him I want to buy this car here. And that you won't let me. See what he says. Oh yeah, tell him that *Mister* Flores is here!"

In that second, I knew I had him. If I'd given him any more talk, he would have called the cops. I know. Or maybe even tossed me out. Old George was a big mother.

44

But when the creep saw me tear up a hundred-dollar bill, he suddenly wasn't so sure of himself. He stood there, looking at me for a second. Then without a word, he turned on his heel and walked over to a sales desk. He picked up the phone, and punched an intercom button, and I heard him say: "Mr. Grober, please."

In a few minutes, a tall skinny guy about Callen's age came out of a back office and into the showroom. Oh man, it was just beautiful! I saw from the expression on old George's face that this had to be Andy Grober, the owner of the agency. The skinny old guy walked past George like he wasn't there. He came up to me and stuck out his hand for a shake.

"Hello there," he said, showing me some teeth so bright and clean that they had to be false. "You must be Freddie Flores. Jack Callen said you might be in. What seems to be the problem, Mr. Flores?"

I looked over Grober's shoulder at George. He didn't miss the *Mister* Flores. Right there, he started to get redder, and I swear, physically smaller. If he could have hidden behind something, I'm sure he would have. But I wasn't going to let him off the hook. I told Grober exactly what had happened, and how George had treated me.

Before you know it, I had my test drive. Then I was in Grober's private office, and he was drawing up a bill of sale for my new car. He gave me a good trade-in on my Olds, and a great discount off the sticker price on the Corvette. I guess he really *did* owe Callen some favors.

The sweetest part was the break I got on price. Grober explained that because old George had frosted me, he was letting me have the car without the salesman's commission!

There was only one problem. The only Corvette they had in stock was the one on the showroom floor. They had to get it off the floor and check it out. It'd take a while. I said I had some clothes to buy, and I'd be home after five o'clock.

"Good, good," Grober said. "By then, the car will be ready to roll. We'll deliver the car to this address ..." he said as he checked my address on the bill of sale," ... that's very close by. And I'd like to apologize to you for any embarrassment you may have had from Mr. Fleischer."

"Is that George's last name? Fleischer?" I asked.

"Yes. He's a good salesman."

"No, he isn't Mr. Grober," I said. "He nearly blew a heavy sale because he judged me wrong. There's lots of working people who have money enough to buy good cars. How many do you figure George has turned away because he didn't like their looks?"

Grober fell silent for a second and then said, "You may be right, Mr. Flores. I have no way of knowing." Then he grinned and said, "But somehow, I think he's not likely to make the same mistake again."

He got up from his desk and shook my hand. "Please say hello to Jack Callen when you see him again, won't you? And if there's anything else I can do for you..."

I had a great idea. "Yes, there is, Mr. Grober," I said. "I'd like a favor, if you would."

"Just name it. That's what we're here for."

"Can you have George deliver the car to me at my house?"

Grober gave me a look that had no name on it. Then, like a volcano erupting, starting with a slow rumble, he began to laugh. It wasn't a put-on laugh, either. It shook his whole skinny frame, and bounced off the paneled walls of his private office.

"I certainly *can* arrange that, Mr. Flores," Grober said, still laughing. "And I think it would be a better lesson than anything I'd say when I chewed him out. Yes, indeed. I'll personally see to it that Mr. Fleischer delivers your new Corvette!"

Being already downtown, I left the Olds in the Grober lot and walked over to where the men's stores are in downtown Santa Amelia. As I crossed the street, I looked back at the showroom. Old George was looking out the window, watching me go. I turned and smiled, then threw him a finger. Whistling a little tune to myself, I went off to buy some new clothes for school.

I had a great time. I bought a dozen Qiana shirts in all colors and prints, and twelve pairs of tightassed slacks. New underwear, new socks, and new everything. Callen was right. The past was over and gone. I even hit one of the pawn shops on Fourth Street. I got myself a gold-filled wristwatch, some rings, and a couple of gold chains with charms on them.

With a new outfit on, I went to a parking lot behind a store. I took the package with my old clothes in it, and was going to throw them in the trash can. Then I saw this old lady.

She was picking through the can I was about to toss my old things into. She was raggedy and she looked dirty. Not the kind of dirty that comes from being a slob, either. This woman looked like she didn't have any place with a bathtub.

I still remember the look on her face when I gave her the bundle of clothes and a five dollar bill. She didn't say thank you. She couldn't. I think she was in shock from a stranger giving her the money.

I don't live far from the downtown area, so I walked home. I shouldn't have done it. I'd bought some new shoes, and I wasn't used to the heels on them. By the time I walked the mile or so to my folks' house, my feet hurt pretty bad. And I had already thrown away my comfortable sneakers. When my doorbell rang, I went to the porch in my socks.

It was George Fleischer, and the new Corvette was sitting in my driveway. George was obviously embarrassed, but he handed me the keys and the papers, saying, "Here's your new car, Mr. Flores."

Now when I say old George was embarrassed, I'm not saying he looked at all *sorry* about the way he had treated me. I know that guys like George don't change. He was sorry that he mouthed off at the wrong Chicano, is all. I could see him all but gag on the *Mister* when he said Mister Flores. So I let him have one more zinger.

I saw that he had driven the Corvette over, and nobody had followed him to drive him back. I was willing to bet that was Andy Grober's doing. Usually, when they deliver a car, they've got either another car following, or a motorbike hooked up to the bumper of the car. That way, the guy who delivers it can get back to the agency. I reached into my pocket and took out a five dollar bill.

"Here's cab fare back," I said with a *Jaws* grin.

Do you know? The mother took it! Had it been me, job or not, I would have tossed the five back in my face. But this huge, redfaced Anglo dude just smiled and said, "Thank you, Mr. Flores." And took the money!

I watched him walk up the street. I didn't know what was going through his mind. But I had a good idea it wasn't pleasant toward Chicanos generally, and one Freddie Flores in particular. I remember thinking: Callen is right. Money makes you different. And money is power.

"VALVERDE ACADEMY HAS BEEN IN existence for seventy-five years," Dean Schuler said. "We accept only one-hundred-fifty students each semester. And of those, many are gone by the end of the term." He stopped and looked pointedly at me. I knew he didn't want an answer or comment. I'd been listening to him run on for over half an hour. Callen was right. This dude was boring!

"We think of ourselves here at Valverde as mid-wives of knowledge in the true Socratic sense," Schuler continued. The drone of his voice subsided into background noise as my attention wandered to the scenery outside the window in Dean Schuler's office.

It was a beautiful place. No doubt about it. Surrounded by trees and set on superbly landscaped grounds. Like Schuler said, there were about five hundred students in the whole place and classes were small. When I drove past the main gate in my new Corvette, I saw students all over the place. And there was no doubt they'd seen me. I saw heads turn and conversations begin as I drove past. I checked it out in my rear-view mirror as I cruised by. I was making an impression.

"Don't you agree?" asked Schuler. I looked back at Schuler with a start. He'd actually stopped talking long enough to expect a response of some sort.

Schuler was a gray man. Just as Jack Callen was pink. His sallow complexion was grayish in tone. He wore a gray three-piece suit, with a gray shirt and a Valverde-pattern tie. It was the only splash of color in his ensemble: maroon and black. A glitter of gold came from a Phi Beta Kappa key that hung from an old-fashioned watch chain across his vest. I was already sure that he wore the suits just to show off the Phi Beta Kappa key. In California, seeing a three-piece suit is on a par with seeing a live dinosaur.

I guess in his way, Schuler is a live dinosaur. He spoke in complete sentences at all times. Some of them had subordinate clauses, like Mr. Johnson had taught us in English back at Santa Amelia High. On occasion, Schuler spoke in italics, too. He had a way of talking that somehow let you hear capital letters and italics. Just now, he was looking at me for a response.

"Most certainly, sir," I said.

"Good. I can see that you understand the *Special Concession* we at Valverde have made in admitting you, despite certain shortcomings in our testing sequences as to your proficiency in Mathematics, young man," he went on and on to say. I wondered what I had just said yes to. But inside, I knew it didn't matter. Schuler is one of those people you agree with. It's easier.

He shuffled some papers on his desk. "Now I see that Administration has placed you in Harbour House. As you may or may not know, upper classmen, er... classpersons, are housed in bungalows on either side of the Arts Building and Little Theater. You will receive a map of the campus from Administration when you leave this office." He consulted his papers again and for the first time since the interview began, he smiled. His teeth were straight. And gray.

"You are *most* fortunate, young man. You have for your roommate one of our most promising students who, I might add, is also Hispanic in origin, though not from the United States. His name is Roderigo Alondra y Castillo, and he is from the Republic of San Martin. I'm sure you will both have a great deal in common; things about which you may chat from time to time. Of course, that would be once your scholastic duties are well completed. We don't encourage socializing at the expense of study here at Valverde, you realize."

My butt was starting to go numb from sitting in the unpadded chair that faced Dean Schuler's desk. I noticed the way he had his office laid out. There were two double windows behind his desk. That meant that at any interview the sun was behind his back and would shine right in the face of anyone he had sitting in the chair. I found out later that the students all referred to it as "being in the hot seat at Schuler's."

I was itching to check into my new place to live. I wondered, too, what this Alondra y Castillo guy was about. From the name, he had to be upper crust in San Martin. Or anywhere Spanish is spoken. When you get a double-handled Spanish name, it means that when the woman married, her family name was too prominent and respected to be dropped. So her unmarried name gets tacked onto the name of her husband.

This Roderigo Alondra y Castillo had to have some family background. See, Castillo means from Castile, in Spain. And if the Alondra family was hot stuff enough to keep their name next to an important name like Castillo...well, you get the idea. But I had to admit, for all the stuffy junk Schuler threw around, it was a nice thing to do. They put me in with another Latino.

"So I'm certain that you will be, as all our alumni have been, a credit to the name of Valverde Academy, young man, and I would like to wish you the best of luck in this new Adventure in Learning upon which you have just now embarked," Schuler said, and put out his hand. I couldn't believe it! He had finally stopped talking! I shook his hand and left the office.

Outside, in the reception area, a secretary gave me a big envelope with my name on it. "You should find all you'll need to know about VV in the indoctrination pamphlet," she said.

"About *what*?" I croaked.

"About VV," she said. "Most of us refer to the school that way. Much shorter than saying Valverde: VV. Get it?"

I'm sure my face was flaming red. I thought that she'd said she'd given me a pamphlet on V.D.! After all, Schuler had told me that the bungalows were coed, and I figured...you know what I figured.

"Oh yeah, VV," I mumbled.

"You've been assigned to Harbour House," she smiled. "You get there by turning left at the corner of this building. Go down Campus Center Drive until you're facing the Music and Art Building, then turn left again. Harbour House is the second bungalow on your left. Have a nice day," she added.

I found the place all right. The secretary's instructions were right on the money. Along the way, I noticed all the stares that my new 'Vette was getting. Good, I thought. Now they know I'm here!

Maybe bungalow wasn't the right word to describe

Harbour House. I mean, the architectural style was pure California contemporary. The bungalow was two stories high, with twenty students and a house parent living inside. The bedrooms, except for the house parent's quarters, were all upstairs. The downstairs had a kitchen, a dining room, and a sitting room. All decorated in VV-stamped or monogrammed stuff. There was a fireplace in the sitting room that you could barbeque a Volkswagen in. A Beetle, not a Rabbit. Definitely a Honda.

I had my two new suitcases that I'd bought at Sears in each of my hands when I entered. I stood in the foyer of the bungalow, looking for someone to give me directions. There was a weirdo sitting in a chair by the unlit fireplace, reading a copy of *National Lampoon*. I mean, he was dressed the opposite of any of the kids I'd seen so far. He had a beard, too. Not much of a beard. He looked kind of like an armpit. With pimples.

I was going to ask the oddball for directions, when someone tapped me on the shoulder. I dropped both my suitcases and I spun around, ready to hit. All I saw was a very startled guy about six feet tall, athletically built. I guess he was maybe eighteen or nineteen. Just then, he was backing away from me, with both hands held waist-high, palms toward me.

"Whooah! You sure are touchy, old son," he said. "I just wanted to tell you that if that Corvette out there is yours, best you move it. The campus cops'll tow it away. And that's for sure."

I felt a small tinge of red begin at my neckline. In my neighborhood, when you're in a strange place and someone taps you on the shoulder from behind, it's usually a setup for a sucker punch when you turn around. I had acted almost reflexively. And scared the hell out of this kid with a Southern accent.

"Sorry, man," I said. "You startled me."

But the blond kid was completely recovered now. I guess my scaring him made him over-react. Since he got himself together, he gave me a real distant look and said, "Parking regulations are strict here at VV. All the help uses the rear entrance and the day-worker parking spaces." He pointed at my luggage. "Best to bring that stuff to the live-in help building, anyway. You won't be sleeping here, you know."

"I won't?" I said. I didn't know what this guy was talking about. But I was beginning to get an idea. One that I didn't care for a great deal, either.

"Ah, you must be Alfredo Flores," said a woman's voice from behind me. "I have your papers all ready. You're in 208, at the end of the corridor. Second floor," the voice concluded.

I saw a look of sheer disbelief come across the blond kid's face as he looked over my shoulder at whoever was talking. I turned and saw this lady of about forty. She was short, blond, and dumpy. She was wearing a tweed suit and those old-lady shoes with low heels on them. And a very warm and friendly smile.

"We haven't met," she said. "I'm the house parent for Harbour House, Mrs. Hargrove. How d'you do?" She gave me a firm, dry handshake. Then to the blond kid, she said, "Lester, I'm afraid you've committed something of a *gaffe*. This is Alfredo Flores. He's a new student. He'll be rooming with Roddie."

"Jeesuhs!" said Lester, "I thought he was the new houseboy!" Then, realizing what he said, he had the good grace to turn bright red. I let it slide. I stuck out my hand and said to him, "Not Alfredo, Freddie. Freddie Flores."

He took my hand like it was a dead rat and mumbled he was sorry and glad to know me. I could tell that I'd already made a potential enemy. I heard a snickery kind of snuffling laugh from the sitting room.

The weirdo had caught the whole action and thought it was real funny. He was sitting straight up in his chair and breaking up like he'd just caught a Steve Martin act. Mrs. Hargrove gave the bearded kid a look that would have frozen a blow-torch. He shut up, and went back to his copy of *National Lampoon*.

"If you'll just follow me, I'll show you to your room," Mrs. Hargrove said, starting up the stairs. I followed. "We have only twenty students in each bungalow," she said over her shoulder. "We at VV always try to place students with others who might share common interests. Your roommate, Roddie, is also Hispanic. He's a delightful young person. I'm sure you'll get along just famously."

"I'm sure," I said with no great enthusiasm.

I don't know what it is with Anglos, but they automatically assume that all Hispanic people have a lot in common. Maybe because we share a language. But all French people don't get along with each other, just because they're French. Look at the French Revolution. They were chopping off heads like crazy back then. And it was Frenchmen doing it to other Frenchmen. But I kept quiet. It's the smartest thing to do when you're on strange turf.

The room was easy half again the size of mine at home. There were two beds, two desks, each with a light fixture. One closet on each side, and an open door that I could see led to a bathroom.

One side of 208 was completely bare and un-adorned. I frowned at the single bed with its VV-monogrammed bedclothes. My bed at home is a three-quarter size. Not that I'm that tall and need the space. I'm five-foot-ten and weigh about one-hundred fifty.

But what caught my eye was the opposite wall. It was covered with pictures of girls. No, not like *Penthouse* or *Playboy*. These were pictures taken by a professional photographer, it looked like. And all the girls in the photos were in bikinis or radically cut bathing suits. And dig this: All of them were

58

autographed "To my dearest Roddie" or "To Roddie with all my love."

Hung from a brace in the ceiling was a color TV with a 19-inch screen and a remote control. I could see from the angle of the set that it was designed to be watched while lying in bed. I thought it was kind of neat.

Taking up all the wall from where the bed ended, up to the window, was a real swell Scandinavian-style wall organizer made out of, I swear, matched-grain rosewood! On its shelves were books that all had fancy bindings and titles in French, Spanish, and German. There were gangs of LP's and a reel-to-reel tape recorder. And dig this: a video cassette recorder!

The bed was neatly made up, and it was covered in an alpaca fur rug coverlet, with alternate black and white squares, like a checkerboard. On the far wall, near where you come in, was a poster-sized portrait of a man in a military uniform. He looked like those guys on TV who are military rulers of Latin American countries: high-peaked officer's cap, a gang of gold braid all over his shoulders and cap, and a chestful of medals. I went over and took a closer look, trying to see if there was a name for this military dude somewhere on the poster.

"That's a portrait of Roddie's father," said Mrs. Hargrove. "Roddie is devoted to his father. You may recognize him. That's Generalissimo Alfonso Alondra y Castillo, president of the Republic of San Martin."

"I thought he looked familiar," I said. Truth to tell, he looked like any of those guys you see on the news when fighting breaks out in Central America. The same guy who is always making speeches to newsmen about restoring law and order and saving the country from communism and Fidel Castro.

"He should look familiar. He's the greatest man in the history of Latin America," said a kid leaning in the doorway.

He was about five-eight. He was wearing designer slacks, a soft cotton shirt with a polo player on it, and a button-up sweater. I could see that this kid worked out with weights. That kind of build is easily spotted. He was wearing cowboy boots with gold filigree. He had a watch on his thick weight-lifter's wrist that was made from a solid gold ingot. I know; I'd seen ads for those watches. He had a chain of heavy gold links around his neck, and on it was one of the most gorgeous Holy Eucharist medals I've ever seen.

"Oh Roddie, I'm so glad you're here!" said Mrs. Hargrove. "You're just in time to meet your new roommate! Roddie Alondra y Castillo, this is Alfr...Freddie Flores. I'm sure you two have many, many things to talk about," she said, brushing at a stray wisp of hair that had come loose from her carefully cemented hairdo. "And I have a million things to do, myself. Oh dear, registration week is such a trial!"

After telling me and Roddie that we should get

to know each other better, Mrs. Hargrove shoved off. We stood looking at each other for a while in silence. Then he came into the room and closed the door. He walked back to where I was standing and spoke in a very low voice, "Listen, Flores, I don't want to raise my voice or cause any fuss. I especially don't want what I have to say overheard. I'm sure you won't, either."

"What's going on, man?" I asked. "Is the room bugged or something?"

See, I didn't know what all the hush-hush was about. I figured that with coed dorms at this place, the whole joint was monitored. I couldn't see any school letting the students mix that way without keeping tabs, somehow.

"Not bugged," Roddie said. "Though it may take a bit of fumigation now that you're here. No, don't bother replying, Flores. What I have to say is brief.

"First off, I do not like you, nor do I have anything in common with you," he said cooly. "We have been thrown together by virtual default. There are only three Latinos at the Academy. We are two of them, though I would hesitate to identify myself with you in any way. The other is a female. Ergo, we have become roommates."

"Then I'll just have that changed," I said.

"This is not a hotel," sneered Roddie. "If it were, you wouldn't be allowed inside. Unless you were wearing a linen coat and carrying a tray. The arrangements are permanent for at least a semester. I have to endure you until next year."

Now, I suppose you're wondering why I didn't just knock this snotty little creep's head off his shoulders. Come to think of it, so do I. But back then, I was so anxious to be accepted, I guess I would have sat still for almost anything. Like what came next in Roddie's little speech.

"The campus is already full of chatter about you, Flores," he said. "Your garish automobile; your sleazy wardrobe and D.A. haircut. You look and carry yourself like something out of *Scarface*. It has taken me three years at this place to convince these folk that all Hispanics don't dress out of horror movies, sleep with their sisters, and take dope. Now you, with your gauche manners, clumsy speech, and gaudy clothing, arrive. Everything I detest being associated with is embodied in you, Flores. And God help me, I must live with it!"

"I love you too, creep," I said. He ignored me and went on.

"So kindly keep to your side of the room. I will not speak to you at all, save when it is necessary, in the dining room. And then, most likely, to remind you not to eat soup with your hands, peon!"

That tore it for me. I got to my feet and grabbed a handful of expensive shirtfront and gritted in his face. "My grandfather was a lawyer, you snot. *Un hombre de onor* and an important man in Mexico. He..."

I never got to finish my sentence. I felt a couple

62

of sharp stabbing pains in my leg and groin. Then before I knew it, I was on my butt, with Roddie standing over me. Evidently he was heavy into the martial arts. He had tossed me around like I was a rag doll. And his hair wasn't even mussed!

"Please don't burden me with your tawdry ancestry, Flores," he said. "I'm amazed you know who your father was, let alone your grandfather. And don't get up, or I will surely break one or two of your bones." He gave a short, barking laugh. "Or see to it that you don't ever propagate your dirty kind. *Adiós*, Flores. Oh, forgive me, I spoke in Spanish. You probably don't speak anything but some gutter dialect."

He turned, and as though nothing had happened, opened the door to our room. He paused in the doorway and said, "By the way. Welcome to Valverde Academy." Then he closed the door silently behind him.

"Yeah," I said to the picture of Roddie's father on the wall. "Welcome to good old VV!"

I WAS STILL SITTING ON THE FLOOR when there was a knock at the door. I figured for sure it wasn't Roddie baby come back for another word. I got to my feet quickly and said, "Come in."

The door opened, and standing there was the weirdo I had seen downstairs in the sitting room. He was a lot taller than I had judged him to be. But then, he had been sitting. He was easy six-foot-four and of medium build.

His big feet were wrapped in scruffy sandals made from tire treads and he wore jeans and a work-shirt that looked slept in. His hair was medium-long and greasy. His toenails needed trimming. Wherever his face wasn't covered by his scraggly beard, it was in full bloom from a case of near-terminal acne.

He smiled, showing me a set of perfect white teeth, the one feature, save for his bright blue eyes, that was appealing.

"I see you've met Snotty Roddie," he said in an Eastern accent. "He's a real charmer, isn't he?"

"A barrel of laughs," I agreed. "I'm..."

"You're Freddie Flores," said the big guy with bad skin. "I heard about you. In fact, the whole school has heard about you. You've already achieved a certain notoriety by grace of your car alone. Oh, I'm sorry, we haven't been introduced. But then again, nobody much speaks to me anyway. I'm Lenny Rosenfeld."

"Glad to know you," I said.

"Don't be too sure you are," Lenny said. "I am what is known as *persona non grata* here at Horrid House. Oldest living student at VV and general all-round pariah. They don't know what to make of me, so they leave me alone. Very alone. Which is just the way I prefer it."

I should have known. The only guy who would talk to me in this upholstered joint would *have* to be the house creep. But considering the other welcomes I'd received from good ol' Lester and Snotty Roddie, I was glad to talk with somebody. Anybody.

"You sure you aren't jeopardizing your social standing by rapping with me?" I asked. Lenny laughed.

65

"I may survive," he smiled. "Which is more than you'll do, if someone doesn't show you the ropes here at beautiful VV."

"It does seem complicated," I admitted. "And I've got off on the wrong foot. I can see that."

"Don't feel bad, Freddie," said Lenny with a wave of a very long-fingered, surprisingly graceful hand. "Nobody gets on with Snotty Roddie. He has a new roomie every semester." Lenny scratched the end of his long, aquiline nose. "Say, can we go down to my room and talk?" he asked. "I can't stand Snotty Roddie's trophies on the wall. My sex life is nil, and I don't need Roddie's gallery to rub it in."

I followed Lenny's lumbering frame down the hall to a room marked 204. The door was covered with "Keep Out" signs and a couple of "Men Working" cards and, in the center, a massive skull and cross-bones. Lenny opened the door, did one of those "after-you" bows, and said, "Welcome to *chez moi*. The last outpost of sensitivity and culture between here and the Pacific Ocean!"

Have you ever seen on "Odd Couple" what Oscar Madison's room looks like? Lenny's place wasn't that neat. All except for one corner. In that corner stood an electric keyboard instrument of some sort. It had all kinds of plugs, jacks, and wires coming out here and going back in there.

On either side of the keyboard were music stands. Framing it all were two speakers so big they looked like they should have been in a movie house. The

66

walls were covered with raunchy old prints and pieces of music manuscripts.

There was a big statue, a bust really, of Johann Sebastian Bach. It stood on the one piece of furniture visible under the general debris: a beautiful table with an inlaid chess board. There was a chess game already set up on it. Lenny noticed me eyeing the setup and asked, "Do you play?"

"A little," I admitted. "My grandfather played. He taught me how. But I haven't played since he died, four years ago."

"Too bad," Lenny said. "I'm brilliant at the game." Just like that, he said it. Like he was saying it looked like rain. But it's the darndest thing. I believed him. This hairy dude may have been the campus creep, but he was no dummy.

"So tell me," I said, once I'd cleared a half-eaten sandwich and an empty soda-pop can from a rickety chair, "just what are the unwritten laws and rules around here?"

"That would take eons to enumerate, my Latin friend," said Lenny, smiling. "But in general, if you do everything in direct opposition to what you've already done, you'll be just fine."

"But what have I done wrong?" I said. "I'm just trying to fit in, is all."

"And failing pitifully in the process," replied Lenny. Seeing my look, he said quickly, "Oh, I'm not trying to put you down, Freddie. I'm trying to help you. That is, if you want help."

"I do," I said. "But if you're the outlaw you say you are, how would you know?"

Lenny smiled. A very nice warm smile. "I didn't say that I *can't* fit in here," he said. "I simply don't *care* to fit in. I don't play their little status games, nor will I be part of anyone's crowd. I have never been part of a pecking order. I consider myself a small islet of culture and humanity, awash in a sea of materialistic barbarity here at VV."

"And to think I was ready for this being a real swell school," I said shaking my head.

"It is. It *is*," Lenny hastened to say. "Scholastically, you can't do better. We have the best facilities, a brilliant faculty, a stiff for a dean. All the requirements for a grade-A prep school."

"Then what's wrong?"

"Everything. It's the attitude of the whole institution. It's a factory that turns out students acceptable in all ways to all good colleges. Getting through VV will virtually guarantee you a pass into any hallowed halls your heart desires."

"I don't see that as so bad," I commented.

"That's because you have no basis for comparison," Lenny said expansively. "I, on the other hand, have been in and out of every platinum-plated prep school from New England through Europe, and finally here."

He reached under a pile of accumulated papers and dirty clothes and produced a warm, unopened can of Pepsi. It opened with a spurt that splashed onto his shirt front, and he quickly stuffed the foaming can into the middle of his beard. The foam ran down the scraggly hairs of his beard and onto his lap. He ignored it.

Lenny wiped his face with the back of his hand, belched elegantly and went on, "And here, we have the full flowering of Southern California culture. Each student, no matter how well off, is striving for still more upward motion, socially. They are all too rich to steal. And having acquired enough pelf —that's money, Freddie—they have been gulled by their parents into pursuing the one thing that can't be bought: Culture. With a capital K!"

"Ah, c'mon Lenny. They can't be all that bad."

"Hell, they can't," Lenny said vehemently. "Except for the minority students, of which I am one..." He raised his eyebrows at me. "Yes, I'm considered a minority student at this place. I'm a Jew. And except for us minorities, the whole damned establishment is a bologna sandwich on mushy white bread with Miracle Whip on it. My God! Haven't you seen your fellow students, Freddie? They all look like Ken and Barbie!"

"Then why do you stay here?" I asked.

"You talk as though I have a choice," smiled Lenny ruefully. "I'm waiting out the time until I turn twenty-one years of age."

"But don't people graduate from here at eighteen?" I asked.

"Some do, I don't. I, for instance, am twenty years, six months and fifteen days old."

"How many minutes?" I grinned.

"I could probably compute that for you, too," Lenny said. "I have a photographic memory and I'm a mathematical genius."

"And have a lot of false modesty," I added. He laughed.

"You're okay, Freddie," he said. "You don't say much, but your utterances are *pithy*."

"Don't *thay* that," I said. "I thought I wath talking thwell." We both laughed. "Besides," I added, "how could anyone get in a word, pithy or otherwise, when you crank up?"

"You're right, of course," Lenny admitted. "But then again, I'm a fascinating conversationalist. Enjoy me while you can. In the next few months, you'll be having conversations with folk for whom 'How are you?' is one of the tough questions."

"I thought you had to be pretty smart to get into Val...er...VV."

"Not at all," Lenny smiled. "You need good grades. That's not the same thing. If you know the simple mechanics of taking examinations, you can have good grades. And you need a good deal of money as well, to enter VV."

"And you have both?" I asked. See, I didn't see how Lenny could be all that rich, if he dressed out of Goodwill.

"I soitenly do, Feniman," said Lenny doing an excellent Groucho. "I am, in fact, the second-richest student at VV. I'm scandalously well off."

"No kidding?" I said. "Who's the richest?"

"You just made his acquaintance," Lenny laughed. "Snotty Roddie is the richest body at VV. While my father merely owns the Melody Corporation of America and Galactic Pictures, its TV subsidiaries and a hotel chain, Snotty Roddie's daddy owns an entire country: San Martin! And they've just struck oil offshore down there. Prior to that, my father could have bought the whole republic for less than half of his holdings in the studio."

"Your dad owns Galactic Pictures?" I gasped. I couldn't believe that this slobby guy was who he was!

"He does now," Lenny said grimly. "Ah, but when I turn twenty-one! That's the delicious part," said Lenny rubbing his hands. "My father won't be the boss any more. When I attain majority, it's in more ways than one. When my mother died, she left me fifty-one percent of Galactic.

"You see, it was a true love match between my folks. She was the studio owner's daughter and my father was an ambitious producer/director. The marriage was made at Bank of America."

I nodded as though I knew what Lenny was talking about.

"But I will have the last laugh," Lenny chortled. "With stock splits and dividends, and Galactic being the parent corporation of all the others...ah, it's going to be sweet when I turn twenty-one."

"I don't understand," I said.

"I suppose not. Corporate law is a labyrinth. Put it this way: my father has been voting my stock proxies since my mother died. He's head of production and chairman of the board. But *only by using my votes*. When I turn twenty-one, I could fire him if I want to! And I *want* to. I can hardly wait!"

"To do your old man dirt?" I asked. "That doesn't seem right. I mean, he's got you in this swell school. I'm sure you get anything you want..."

"Jail!" snorted Lenny. "He's shipped me from one gold-plated jail to another for as long as I can remember. Anyplace far enough away so that he can have his swinging time with would-be actresses, whose only talents are physical. He's a woman-crazy old goat! He broke my mother's heart. She committed suicide, Freddie. And when I get control of the corporation, he's going to pay for it!"

Abruptly, the vicious look left Lenny Rosenfeld's face. He gave me a big, warm grin. "My family tree has termites," he said softly. "But that isn't what you asked about. You wanted to know how to act around here, didn't you?"

"I sure did."

"My immediate question is, why conform? But far be it for me to force my lifestyle on anyone. Sure I'll help you, Freddie. But it *will* give me a slight case of moral indigestion." He looked at me and said, "Stand up." I did. "Turn around." I did.

"No doubt about it, you have it all together for a low-class disco night out," he said. Oddly enough,

72

it didn't make me mad. It was the way he said it. For all his nasty mouth, this big, sloppy guy had a good heart.

"I bought the best I could," I offered in my own defense.

"Then you're shopping in the wrong places," Lenny answered. "Once you get settled in and class schedules are worked out, we'll get in that juke box you're driving and go shopping."

"But I spent all my clothing money," I protested. "I'd have to call up my guardian to get more money."

"So? That's no big deal."

"But what'll I tell him? He just gave me money for new stuff."

"As I understand it, from what I've read in the papers, you are able to attend this place because of your family's untimely demise, isn't that so?"

"Yeah!" I said in wonder. "But how did you know?"

"I told you. I have a photographic memory. I read about that plane crash in Mexico a couple of months ago. And there was a follow-up story on you becoming a ward of the court and your new-found fortune. Obviously, there aren't that many Alfredo Floreses around. And you turning up at VV would seem natural enough. Elementary, my dear Flores."

I whistled a tuneless whistle. "You are smart, aren't you?" I said.

"A genius, actually," Lenny conceded. "But in any event, you have a guardian. Freddie, you don't answer to him. He answers to you! You just call and tell him you bought clothes that were all wrong for this place. He'll understand. And if he doesn't, I'll take the phone."

"I...don't know..." I began.

"Exactly!" Lenny crowed. "You don't know. And I do! If you want to fit in around here, and I can't understand why, I know all there is to know. Place yourself in my hands, Freddie. I'll make you a Big Man on Campus by Christmas!"

"You'll forgive a non-genius for inquiring," I said. "But tell me, Lenny. Why should you do all this for me? You don't know me from a hole in the ground. And you don't seem to care, so long as I listen to you. Why? Just tell me why and maybe I'll go along with you."

Lenny leaned back in his chair and laced his fingers behind his head. "It would take a long time to explain. Part of it is my doing a Pygmalion trip. I'll be honest with you about that. But that's not the main reason."

"And what is?"

Lenny suddenly leaned forward and his nose wasn't inches from mine. I could smell he had a vaguely sour odor to him. He spoke in a low voice that had an edge of case-hardened steel to it.

"Because I thoroughly loathe and despise Roderigo Alondra y Castillo and everything he stands for. Anyone with an atom of taste or intelligence would. I know he hates you. I listened at the door when he gave you his little pep talk."

"You eavesdropped?"

"Absolutely. One of my favorite pastimes. Anyway, I'd like to see you shove an umbrella up Señor Castillo and open it. Socially speaking, that is. Don't fool with him physically. He's dangerous."

"I found out."

"Well, don't think you can wait for him outside the gates and get even, either. Once he goes outside the gates, his father's hired goons follow him like Secret Service. You might have seen them in that Caddie limo outside the gate."

"I didn't notice."

"They're there, believe me."

"I'll remember."

"Good. Now, like I say, there's still another reason I want to help you here."

"Which is?"

"You're not yet ravaged by the system. You're still a real person. I sort of like your style, Freddie. Is that reason enough?" He stuck out his hand, and I shook it. I noticed it was sticky from the spilled soda pop. I didn't mind.

LENNY SURE WAS RIGHT ABOUT HOW busy I'd be over the next two weeks. I thought that this school would be a little different from my old high school. Mostly, because the buildings were more elaborate and the equipment newer. But it was more than that.

Like Lenny told me, the aim of Valverde is to get their students accepted by major colleges. So they don't set up everyone with the same classes. They concentrate on your weakest subjects, and they also give you extra, more advanced work in your good ones. For instance, art is my strongest subject. It was because of that I went to my first life class.

A life class is where you have a real live model

who poses for you. I'd only seen stuff like that in movies on TV. Like, I saw one where Tony Franciosa played the Spanish painter Goya. It was called *The Nude Maja*. Tony painted two pictures of Ava Gardner in the flick. One with clothes on, one without. The trouble came when Ava's old man wanted to know about the picture he did *without* her clothes on.

Anyhow, I got all my materials together and went over to the big building that had the art studios and the theater in it. Man, they do it right at good old VV. The classrooms had skylight windows and one whole wall of glass that let in only north light. North light is the best natural light to work in. The angle of the sun remains constant.

I found out how important that is when I met Mr. Schwartzberg, the art teacher. The same color can look different in different light. And if you want your work to be consistent in color, you have to do it all in the same kind of light. Otherwise your colors get all screwed up.

It was my first time in life class, and I was wondering what it would be like. I didn't have to wonder long. The studio was all set up for charcoal sketching. Easels and worktables were in a semicircle around an elevated platform. We were all given assigned work areas, and just before we were ready to begin, Mr. Schwartzberg got up and gave us a little speech.

Mr. Schwartzberg is a tall, thin man, who looks

like he only eats once a week. He's about fifty years old and nearly completely bald. Some of the kids call him Onion Head on account of his shiny head of skin.

He's in the wrong line of work, too. I mean, he's a swell artist and all. I know that some of his paintings are in the Museum of Modern Art in New York City. But when he talks, he stutters. It could be that when someone's an artist, his work speaks for him.

"St-st-students," he said, "t-today we will be wor-wor-working with a l-l-live model."

A woman of about thirty, with red hair tied up in a bun, and wearing a bathrobe and rubber sandals, came out. She walked to the little stage I told you about. "This is Mmmm-ms. Lester," Schwartzberg said. She will pose standing for this session. Are you r-r-ready?" he asked the redheaded woman. She nodded.

Then dig what happened: this Ms. Lester takes off the bathrobe. I expected she'd be wearing a leotard or tights. *Something*, at least. But man, Ms. Lester was stark, staring naked!

Now, this may sound like I'm some kind of turkey, but I never in my life had seen a woman without a stitch of clothing on. Oh sure, I've seen pictures in the girlie magazines. But right there, in the flesh, was a grown woman wearing nothing but a slightly bored expression on her face. I was so stunned by it all that I know my mouth dropped open!

I know it dropped open, because as I stood there agape, from alongside me this *hand* came out and with fingertips, closed my open yap. I gave a start, and looked over to my right, where the mysterious hand had come from. I found myself looking into the face of one of the most beautiful black girls I'd ever seen.

She was about two inches shorter than me, and her skin was a soft, velvety brown. She was smiling at me with a smile that could have lit up the studio. Her eyes, with long lashes, were slightly turned up at the corners, giving her an exotic, almost Oriental look. Right then, though, she wasn't looking all that exotic. She was trying very hard not to laugh out loud at my reaction to the naked lady in front of us.

"That's nothing," she said to me, grinning, "you haven't lived until you've seen it in basic black!"

"I...uh...guess so," I said brilliantly.

"P-p-pay at-at-tention, over there," I heard from Onion Head. I looked up in embarrassment. He was staring pointedly at me and this gorgeous black chick. I must have turned red.

I got down to business then, paying all my attention to the naked lady model. And it was the weirdest thing. After the initial shock wore off, I began to realize how important a live model can be to someone studying art.

I think I said early on that I had trouble with hands. I found out why. In the past, when I'd drawn people, I had always drawn them with clothes on. I mean, their extremities came from, and grew out of, their clothes. Seeing this naked lady move once in a while, and by shifting the angle I looked at her from, I saw where I'd been going wrong.

All the art texts that I'd seen with anatomical sections in them were fine. But they were *static*. In order to draw the human body, you must see how it works in *motion*. A drawing or a painting is the capturing of a moment in time.

But it's to be remembered that when you paint or draw a body at rest, that there is motion throughout. The model may not be moving a hair, but there is always the potential for motion there. I don't know if that's clear, but it's the best I can say it.

Anyhow, it all came together for me that day, with the naked lady. Onion Head came up behind me while I was sketching, and I was so into what I was doing that I didn't even notice him until he spoke up.

"That is truly f-f-fine w-w-ork, F-flores," he said to me. "I-d l-l-like to t-t-talk with you after cl-cl-class." Then he walked over to the black chick's work. "Also very g-g-good, Ms. Simpson," he said.

So that's her name, I thought: Simpson. I couldn't help but wonder where she was living. If she was an upper classperson, as Dean Schuler puts it, she probably had a room in one of the bungalows. I was kind of let down when she took off as soon as the bell rang to signal the end of the life class. I would have followed her, but I'd already said that I would speak with Mr. Schwartzberg afterwards.

My regret went away once I heard what he had to say. And you know what? He only stammers that bad when he talks in front of people. When we talked later that day, he hardly stuttered at all.

He was at his desk, in a corner of the studio, when I went over to him. He was completely wrapped up in what he was doing. I had to clear my throat to get his attention. He looked up and seemed startled that I was there. Then he gave me a big smile and said, "Ah, F-flores, I'm glad you stayed. I'd l-like to s-speak to you about your work."

And speak he did. For a man with a speech impediment, he did run on. Not that I'm complaining. It's very hard to be impatient with a man who spends fifteen minutes telling you how talented you are. And baby, that's just what he did.

He asked me if I'd ever worked in oils. I told him no; we couldn't afford that kind of outlay at my house. His eyebrows went up when I told him that. I saw that I had to explain to him about how I was at VV to begin with.

After I finished telling him my tale of woe, he looked at me and ran a long, bony hand over his shiny head.

"Freddie, you have a talent. And you have a responsibility to develop it. It's difficult to explain," he said. "Essentially, one works in art because one

81

has no choice. I could never be anything but an artist. Not because I can't do other things. I teach, for instance. It's an inner need, being an artist... a need for expression.

"My teaching post allows me to do my own work. It also allows me to find true talent, if it should happen to show up in my classroom. I feel that in your case, it has. I can see that need in your work. That's why I feel you should pursue a career in art."

"Excuse me, sir," I said. "I don't mean any disrespect. But you've only seen one thing I've done... the sketch from the life class. How could you tell I might be good?"

Schwartzberg smiled. "Have you ever heard of Giotto?" he asked.

"No, sir."

"Giotto was an Italian thirteenth-century painter. His father apprenticed him into the wool trade, in Florence. The wool shop was near the workshop of Cimabue, then the greatest painter in Italy. Young Giotto couldn't keep his mind on the wool business. He kept haunting Cimabue's studio.

"One day, Cimabue asked Giotto the reason. Giotto told him that he wanted to be a painter. Cimabue handed the boy a piece of paper and a stick of charcoal. 'Draw something,' he commanded. Giotto drew a circle on the paper."

"That was it?" I asked. "Just a circle?"

"Hardly," said Schwartzberg, with a smile. "It was a *perfect* circle. It was enough to convince

82

Cimabue. He spoke with Giotto's father. Soon, Giotto was Cimabue's student. Today, the world doesn't remember Cimabue. But Giotto is revered as the father of modern art.

"So, Freddie, I don't need to see a whole portfolio of your work. Your single figure study was enough for me to tell. Now, tell me. Where do you intend to follow your art career? What school?"

I had to tell him that I was preparing for Stanford. And like Callen's grandson, I was going for business administration.

"In the n-name of G-god, why?" Schwartzberg asked. "You're an artist, boy! Examine your goals. I wait patiently, each year, to find a real talent in one of my classes. I have cranked out a succession of daubers and Sunday painters. Now, someone with real ability walks in, and tells me he wants to be some sort of b-bookkeeper! You have a chance to be something rare and wonderful, Flores. Don't throw it away!"

We talked more, and I promised Schwartzberg I'd think about it. I left the studio on cloud nine. Me, a real artist! True, Mr. Landesman, my art teacher at Santa Amelia High, told me I had talent. He said maybe I could get a job as a commercial artist. But Mr. Schwartzberg was saying something entirely different.

I think I knew why, too. Landesman knew who I was, and my background. He knew I'd never get a chance to study wherever I wanted, and I guess he figured a commercial art job was the best I could hope for. Now, it was different. Now, I had the money. And Mr. Schwartzberg said I had the talent. I walked on air all the way to my bungalow.

My high didn't last long. Back at Harbour House, or Horrid House, as Lenny calls it, I had a real problem. Snotty Roddie.

I had discovered why he kept the video recorder in his room. The slimy little creep had a collection of porno tapes that he played on the machine. Now, I'm not knocking how anyone else gets off on life. I figure you do what you do; I do my thing. But these tapes were different. They were kinky.

I also discovered that my math was a lot weaker than I had thought. I had to study and study hard just to keep up with the rest of the kids in my classes... yeah, classes. I had two different math courses that I had to take. Each one was three hours a week. And with the constant distraction of Snotty Roddie's videotape player going, it was near-impossible to study in the room we were forced to share.

Man, it's hard enough to study at stuff you *like*, when there's a heavy distraction. And I admit it; I don't like math. So there I was, trying to get down the binomial theorem, and Snotty Roddie was playing his dirty movies.

To make it worse, he had the sound hooked up to his stereo. So all I heard, even when I turned my desk away from the video screen, were sighs

84

and moans. And lots of heavy breathing.

What could I do? I couldn't report what Snotty Roddie was doing. I could hate him all I wanted, but I'm no rat. I wouldn't blow the whistle, even on a creep like Roddie. Then again, I'd flunk out of VV if I didn't do *something*.

It was Lenny Rosenfeld who came to my rescue. I was sitting in Lenny's room, rapping about the problem. We were also making plans for the shopping expedition to get me some clothes.

"Look, Freddie," Lenny had said, "why don't you move your study stuff in here? Into my room? I've got the space."

I laughed. "You do, huh?" I said. "You can't prove it by me. I've been in this room maybe fifty times. I've never seen the floor."

"That's nothing," Lenny said with an airy wave of his hand. "I can condense the debris onto one side of the room. And by the way, you misunderstand the nature of this," he said, indicating the huge mess that was his room. "There is organization amid what, on the surface, appears to be chaos."

"Sure, sure."

"I'm serious," Lenny protested. "I told you. I have a photographic memory. People with poor memories have filing systems. I don't need one. I remember where I put everything. And anything I want, I can put my hands upon immediately."

As though to prove his point, Lenny got up and began rummaging through a big pile of dirty laundry and papers. He snaked his hand under the pile and produced a warm can of Pepsi. "See?" he said, with a grin.

And that's how I came to be spending more time in Lenny's place than in the room I shared with Snotty Roddie. Lenny was as good as his word. When I showed up the next day, I couldn't believe it. The whole room was absolutely spotless, and all the stuff was put away.

"Voila!" Lenny said, as I walked into the room. "An antiseptic *atelier* for our budding Cezanne!"

"But Lenny," I said in wonder, "how'd you do it? It looks great in here! But what happened to all your junk?"

"I told you that I don't need a filing system," he said, getting up and walking over to a closet. "I simply reorganized things."

He opened the closet door, and about a half-ton of books, laundry, papers, magazines, and LP's fell out onto the floor. He looked at me with a smile and said, "Would you believe that I know where every last item is in this mound of material?"

"No," I said.

"You may be right," he laughed.

I didn't care. I had my study space, and even enough room to set up my drawing board and easel. All I needed to use my other room for was to sleep in. Which is how it worked out. I made a half-dozen trips down the hall to move my stuff.

Snotty Roddie was up watching his dirty movies

when I got in. We hadn't spoken a word since that first day, except at the dinner table downstairs. At dinner, because Mrs. Hargrove sat at the table with us, he was so nicey-nice, you could have puked. He was all chit-chat about school activities and talked politics, especially Latin American politics.

Say what you want about Snotty Roddie. You won't say anything I haven't, and worse. But he is a sharp little mother. He knows economics, international politics . . . you name it. If it has to do with administration of a government, he's got it down to a tee. And then some.

It's true that Roddie is being groomed to take over the government of San Martin when his father retires or dies. And Snotty Roddie will be ready.

And that's not all I was learning. Mrs. Hargrove says that for wealthy children, we all had terrible table manners, except for Roddie. I knew that before I ever came to VV. First time they sat me down in the Horrid House dining room, I'd never seen so many knives, forks, and spoons just to eat one meal! I was ready to watch everyone else and do what they did. Turned out I didn't have to. Mrs. Hargrove made every meal at Horrid House a little lesson in etiquette. Before long, I was eating as classy as Snotty Roddie.

The thing that vaguely bothered me was being served dinner by the houseboy. I don't know what I would have done if he had been a Latino. Many of the houseboys at VV are. Our houseboy was Vietnamese and his name was Dong. No kidding, that's his name. But even so, I felt funny being served.

One night in particular, I finally got a word in edgewise on Snotty Roddie. He was holding forth on art. To hear him talk, you'd think he was the ultimate authority on everything. The worst part is, he's almost always right in his pronouncements.

"Ah, the Fabergé collection," he was saying that night, "I have seen my father's few works by Fabergé. He has some pieces that once belonged to the last czar of Russia. One or two of the Easter eggs. There's no doubt that Fabergé was one of the master jewelers of all time."

"Not a jeweler," I said.

"I beg your pardon, Mr. Flores," he said, making the word *mister* sound like an insult. "Did I hear you express an opinion on Fabergé? But then of course, you probably wear some cheap cologne that bears that name..."

"Roddie!" squawked Mrs. Hargrove. "How rude of you! I'm surprised at you. Just because Mr. Flores may not be as widely traveled as you are..."

"It's all right, Mrs. Hargrove," I said easily. "Mr. Castillo was referring to Peter Karl Fabergé. Nineteenth- and twentieth-century artisan. It's true that Fabergé worked in precious metals and stones, but even Fabergé himself called his work art objects. To call Fabergé a jeweler is like calling Benvenuto Cellini a silversmith."

88

"Very good!" said Mrs. Hargrove. "You see, Roddie? You misjudged Mr. Flores' meaning."

I couldn't resist one more shot, and I took it. "As to the scent in the room we share, Mr. Castillo," I said evenly, "it's simply soap and water. But coming from Central America as you do, that's probably why you had trouble identifying it."

If looks could kill, I would have been dead on the spot. If Snotty Roddie had been back home in San Martin, he would have had me in front of a firing squad by dawn. I didn't care. I had beaten Roddie at his own game. Score one for the Chicano kid from Santa Amelia!

I guess Roddie had been stewing about it since then. When I came back from Lenny's room that night, he spoke to me. "Now that you're becoming a dinner table wit, Flores, I must caution you. I never forget a slight or an insult."

I didn't say anything. I just got into bed and snapped off my bedlamp. Roddie kept the video player going. I raised up on one elbow and said, "Castillo?"

"Yes?"

"Sit on it!"

8

I LOOKED AT MYSELF IN THE MIRROR
and couldn't believe it was Freddie Flores. I was in
Lorenzo's on Rodeo Drive in Beverly Hills. If you've
never been in any of the expensive shops on Rodeo
Drive, let me just say that change for a dollar costs
five bucks there.

"What do you think, Freddie?" Lenny said.

"It looks like someone I vaguely recognize, but
that's all," I said, pointing to my reflection in the
mirror. I was wearing a set of dark wool slacks, a
white Italian knit turtleneck, a gray suede sports
coat, and Gucci loafers. What made me look even
less like myself was the haircut.

Lenny had taken me to Signor Guido's, where I

90

had been shampooed, cut, and styled. I was blow-dried and powdered, cologned and hairsprayed. I felt like a horse's butt when they'd done all that fussing over me.

I had to admit, though, as I looked at myself, that I was a guy who could go anywhere. And get good service when I did. What puzzled me at first was Lenny. He didn't dress any different in Beverly Hills than he did at VV. But with him, it didn't matter.

Soon as we walked into any of the half-dozen shops we'd visited, the salespeople bowed down like he was a king. They all knew him by sight and knew his name. And Lenny accepted it the same way he took everything at Valverde. He shambled around, looking like a slob and saying things so clever that most people missed what he was driving at.

What knocked me out, too, was that whenever we bought some stuff, Lenny would have the dude that worked at the store bring the merchandise out to my car. The Corvette was full to bulging with clothes and accessories we'd bought.

Lenny had been right about Callen, too. When I told him on the phone that I was dressed all wrong for VV, he understood right away. I'd expected some hesitancy on his part when I told him that five hundred dollars wouldn't be near enough. Lenny had told me to get a thousand, which is what I did.

Callen never turned a hair. I got the check in the

mail two days after I talked to him on the phone.

I know this may grab you as hard to swallow: inside of an hour and a half of shopping in Beverly Hills, the whole thousand bucks was gone! I was ready then to go back to VV but Lenny said I wasn't near finished. He opened his wallet and showed me a string of credit cards.

"Not to worry, Freddie," he said. "I have those little bits of plastic that make life worthwhile. It's my father's money. Let's spend it!"

And so we did. In stores I'd never heard of. But Lenny knew about them. By the time we were done, the whole back storage area of my car was crammed with fancy clothes and extra stuff. We had lunch at a restaurant called Le Bistro. They stuck us way in back when they got a look at Lenny. I guess you can get away with just so much, looking like a slob. Even a very rich one.

Over a spinach quiche, Lenny said to me, "You're set now, Freddie, for any occasion. All you need is to get a VV patch for that Cardin blazer we bought, and no one at Valverde can fault you for what you wear. Or how you look."

"Listen man," I said. "There's a lot about you that puzzles me."

"Like what?" He smiled, showing bits of spinach in his teeth. Lenny is a terrible eater.

"Like how you know everything that's exactly right to wear. How all the help at these fancy stores know you. Yet you always dress out of an army surplus store."

He laughed. "Just because I'm not playing the game doesn't mean I don't know the rules, Freddie. I must confess, that at one time, I looked pretty much like your typical VV student. I wore the right clothes ... hell, I wouldn't even dress out of Beverly Hills in those days. I got my outfits in New York, London, and Paris."

"Geez, Lenny, What happened to you?"

"Look at him," Lenny said, with a sardonic grin. "Give the kid a decent set of clothes and he starts snubbing his old pal Lenny. I suppose you'd like me to start dressing up to keep you company now?"

"Aw c'mon, Lenny," I protested. "You know what I'm getting at."

"Yes, I do. Just having a little joke, is all," he said. He picked up a breadstick from the holder on the table and began swabbing out the little pot the quiche had come in.

"Once I was your fashion hound," he told me. "But when my mother died ... I lost heart. I looked at my father, who I think takes showers with a tie and shirt on, and saw what I hated most. My mother had always been impressed with Harry's clothes and his impeccable style."

"Harry being your father?"

"You got it, champ. Yeah, Harry is right out of the pages of *Gentlemen's Quarterly*. I looked at Harry, thought about my poor mom, and something snapped inside me. I haven't worn a tie since."

93

He finished the bread stick and began sucking at his teeth. "Is there any other skeleton in the Rosenfeld family closet you'd like rattled?" he asked archly.

"Yes, now that you volunteer," I said. "How come when every other kid at VV has a roomie, you don't? And rich as you are, how come you don't have a car, either? And how come you always eat in your room? I thought we had to eat in the dining room."

"You are inquisitive today, aren't you?"

"No, no. It's all right, Lenny," I said. "I wasn't trying to snoop into your private life. It's just that, well, I *like* you. I want to know more about you. God knows, I've told you all about myself. My *abuelo*, my dad, Callen, the works. But I really don't know you, close as we are."

"It's a long, dreary tale, I'm afraid," Lenny sighed. "But as briefly and concisely as possible, I'll answer your questions. First, about eating and living alone. Have you been inside the theater at VV?"

"Sure I have. It's beautiful," I replied, wondering what that had to do with my questions.

"Have you noticed the brass plaque in the lobby?"

"Yeah," I said. "It's the Benjamin Levinson Theater."

"Named for Ben Levinson, founder of Galactic Pictures, and also my maternal grandfather," Lenny said. "Do you begin to get the picture?"

"I think so..."

"There's more," said Lenny, with a sardonic grin.

94

"The whole idea of Ben Levinson donating a legitimate theater, for stage plays, is a joke. Ben's bad movies probably set back the dramatic arts more than any other studio's films. Old Ben must have thought they were going to show *movies* in his memorial theater!"

"But it's a beautiful theater."

"For sure, Freddie, for sure. That was Harry's doing. See, Harry came upon the scene when Galactic was in trouble. TV was knocking studios out of business right and left. He saw that the trend in motion pictures was toward quality. And let TV show the grade-B stuff."

Lenny paused and called over a waiter, who descended on us with the deference that only the very rich get from waiters in a French restaurant.

"*Vous desirez, M'sieur?*" asked the waiter.

"*Une tasse de café filtre, avec un petit peau de citron,*" Lenny said to the waiter. And to me, "You want coffee, too?"

I nodded yes, and Lenny continued after the waiter left, "So Harry sold TV rights to all the schlocky movies Ben Levinson had churned out during the thirties and forties. Made a fortune, too.

"At that time, the studios were trying to ignore TV, hoping it'd go away. Harry turned all his attention to making quality films. Harry has a little taste," Lenny smiled, "which as George S. Kaufman once said, is easily distinguished from no taste at all."

95

"What's that got to do with the theater at VV?"

"I'm coming to that. Harry's films won Oscars, something that Ben's had never done. All of a sudden, Galactic had 'kulcher.' Ben began thinking of himself as a patron of the arts. Then Harry, who, incidentally, went to Valverde, talked the old man into donating the theater."

"So that donation gives you a lot of special privileges?"

"A million and a half bucks worth of 1961 dollars buys a lot of privilege, Freddie," Lenny admitted. "Plus Harry is always good for a heavy contribution each year."

"Okay, I got you. You eat alone because you..."

"Because I can't stand to be at the same table with Snotty Roddie," said Lenny vehemently. "I have the clout to get away with eating alone, and I use it."

"What about no car, then?" I asked. "That hasn't got to do with privileges at VV."

"No it doesn't," Lenny smiled ruefully. "It has to do with when my mother died. I went nuts. I was just sixteen and Harry had a brand-new Jaguar. I got myself all doped up on speed, booze, and smoke and wrapped myself and the Jag around a family car full of kids on the San Diego Freeway.

"One of them died. I lost my license. Once I had been detoxified, I swore I'd never drive again. I haven't either. Now you know my whole sordid tale. Can we go now?"

We finished up and paid the check. On the drive back to Valverde, Lenny didn't say a word. I didn't push it, either.

I understood where Lenny was coming from, especially about the dope thing. It's part of the reason I don't mess with any kind of dope. I lost a good friend that way. When I was only twelve.

My best friend was a kid named Billy Ramos. When he was just twelve, he began fooling around with dope. He wanted to look hip and older, run with the heavies in the neighborhood.

One afternoon, he dropped a bunch of acid, LSD. Convinced he could fly, he jumped off the roof of his parent's garage. He landed on his head and broke his neck and skull. He died on the way to the hospital.

That's why I don't have anything to do with acid, speed, or booze. Even cigarettes or weed. One gives you cancer; the other makes you crazy.

Dope is a fact of life in my old neighborhood. You know it's always there, and that a lot of people do it. Maybe they can handle it. They say they can. But poor Billy thought he could handle it, too. Look where he ended up. In a grave.

I found out a lot about Lenny that day we went shopping. I was also beginning to have some idea of what really went on at VV. There was a whole lot of politics I didn't dream existed. I was soon to find out *just* how tangled up politics were at Valverde Academy. It cost me a lot to find out, too.

97

9

AROUND THANKSGIVING TIME, THE school emptied out. It seemed that everyone had a special place to go, family to be with, and a swell holiday planned. Except me. I had no place in particular, nor any desire to do something special.

It would be my first Thanksgiving without a family. Sure, Mrs. Fernandez had asked if I was coming home. But what would I come home to? I didn't even have any friends left in Santa Amelia.

I hadn't made any plans and hadn't talked to anyone about Thanksgiving, not even Lenny. I guess I figured if I didn't pay attention to it, the holiday would go away.

But VV was like a ghost town. If you rolled a

bowling ball down Campus Center Drive it would have gone all the way across the Quad and not hit anyone. Even Snotty Roddie was off someplace. Maybe San Martin; I wouldn't know, and I sure didn't care. I was enjoying my room for the first time since I'd come to Valverde Academy.

I hadn't seen Lenny in a day or so. I naturally assumed that he was gone. I was working on a drawing in my room, kind of a daydream castle, when I heard the sounds. Strange, tortured sounds, but they were somehow appealing. Have you ever seen a science fiction movie where the music can make your skin crawl? That's the kind of thing I mean.

I went out of my room and down the corridor, listening for the source of the eerie sounds. The doors were all closed, and I listened at each one. I knew that everyone in the Horrid House menagerie was away. Not that I mixed socially with anyone but Lenny.

Lenny had been right about the students, generally. The girls at Horrid House were all nice, but somehow like vacant houses. All the exterior was there. But any time I'd tried to talk to them, they frosted me. Those that did talk didn't say zilch.

I'd seen Natalie Simpson, the black chick, in my art classes. She had a lot to say, but each time I'd tried to get closer to her, she put me off. Always in a very nice way, you dig, but a putoff, just the same.

We went to a couple of art films on campus together, and we got to be tight on a superficial level. However much I pushed, though, there was just so far you could go talking with Nat. Then she'd shut down. I even came right out and asked her about it. Her answer really rocked me.

I was walking her back to her bungalow, Brice House. We'd talked mostly about the movie we'd seen. It was on Alexander Calder, the guy who did all those wild mobiles. Then one of those silences happened. You know, when two people both run out of things to say at the same time? It was then I came right out and said, "Nat, you know I like you a whole lot, don't you?"

"I got that message, Freddie. I like you, too."

"Then how come it never goes past that?" I asked. "We go to films. We even went to the welcome dance together. But Nat, it's like there's a little inner wall you have. Each time I try to get close, up comes that wall. What is it? Is it the way I used to dress? Or maybe something I said?"

"Oh Freddie," she said and grabbed my hand hard. "You're so together some ways. In others, you're a child."

"Meaning what?"

"Haven't you noticed?" she asked. "I'm black."

"And I'm Chicano. What's that to me?"

"Nothing at all. And that's probably the best part of your character. But I can't afford to get involved with you. And God help me, I could. Very easily."

"Then what's wrong?" I demanded. "You feel you're stepping down socially taking up with me?" I was getting steamed. In fact, I was going to say more, but as we passed a street lamp, I saw she was crying!

"Hey, wait a minute, Nat," I began. "If it's going to put you through changes..."

"Oh damn!" she said suddenly. "It's not you. It's me. It's my family...all they've worked for...I can't...I..."

I couldn't help it. I gathered her up in my arms and gave her a long, lingering kiss. At first, she pulled back. Then all of a sudden, she was in my arms like she belonged there. I was just getting used to the feeling when she abruptly pulled away from me. She shook her head, the way you sometimes see a prizefighter do when they've been hit hard.

Then she looked me straight in the eye and said, "Freddie, it's not you. It's my responsibility to my family. The Simpsons have been in this part of California for generations. My ancestors were never slaves. They were freemen. The ones that weren't Chinese, that is. In black society, we're upper crust. I'm at Valverde to sharpen up for my college boards, that's all. It isn't necessary, really. I know my work cold. It's just the cachet of being a Valverde graduate that gives one an extra edge."

"Swell, but what's that got to do with you and me?"

"I am expected to follow certain family traditions,

that's all. I am going to be a lawyer. And a good one, too. Just like my mother is."

"No kidding?" I exclaimed. "My grandfather was a lawyer too. In Mexico."

"Stop it, stop it!" she cried. "Will you stop being so nice and understanding? I have something to say to you!"

"Okay, okay. Not another word," I promised.

"Right. Freddie, I could love you, I really could."

"Nat!"

"Will you shut up?" she snapped. "You promised!"

I shut up.

"But as much as I care for you, Freddie," she continued, "I can't get involved with you. This may sound corny and old-fashioned, but I'm a virgin, Freddie. I've never given myself to any boy or man. I don't come cheap. With me, it's got to be the whole setup: husband, home, family, and my career in law."

"Great with me!" I said. "I got money, I can help you..."

"Freddie, Freddie," she said and put her hand on my cheek. "*I* have money. Lots and lots of money. It's the entrance card at VV to have money. There are no poor scholarship students at Valverde. My folks own real estate all through the San Fernando Valley. My father is president of the biggest black bank in California. I had a society *debut*, for God's sake! No, it's not money. It's race, Freddie. You're wonderful, you're sensitive, you're talented. But darling, you just aren't black."

I couldn't hear anymore. What a joke! Here, I'd played the game. I got the haircut and wardrobe. I was dropping *bon mots* at the dinner table and getting the best of Snotty Roddie once in a while. But the one woman I cared for was turning me down. Because I wasn't black! After all the time and money I'd spent being as white as anyone at Valverde!

My *abuelo* always told me, only those you love can hurt you. You don't let enemies get close enough. Abuelo was right. Before Natalie could see what was written plainly on my face, I turned and ran for Horrid House.

"Wait, Freddie!" she called after me. "You don't understand!"

"The hell I don't!" I cried over my shoulder.

I ran all the way back to Horrid House. When I got in, Snotty Roddie wasn't in the room. I had almost hoped he would be. I wanted to hit something. Break something. And karate or not, I was ready to deal with Roderigo Alondra y Castillo that night!

I had brooded about the scene with Natalie for two days, and then the Thanksgiving holiday came. I was glad. I couldn't bear to see her in the life class.

Which is how I came to be alone in Horrid House, listening at doors, trying to find where the strange music was coming from. I got all the way down to Lenny's room before I realized that the sounds were coming from there. I listened to make sure, then knocked at the door. No answer. I guess the music was too loud inside. I opened the door.

Lenny was sitting at the electronic keyboard I'd seen in the room, but had never heard him play. He was dressed only in a set of headphones, which were connected to the octopus of wiring that grew out of the tangle of electronic equipment. That's why he hadn't heard my knock: the headset he was wearing. I came into the room and listened for a while. Lenny didn't know I was there. He was completely into his music.

It was weird, all right. But that music was haunting as well. Every time it started to get real pretty and lyrical, Lenny would push some kind of button at the console, and the music would take another, stranger turn. I didn't disturb him.

Finally, he finished his outer-space concert and turned halfway around, but still not far enough to see me.

"Hi, Freddie," he said.

"How did..."

"Elementary, my dear Flores," he said, turning around fully to face me. "We're the only ones left at Horrid House. The help wouldn't dare come in here. They think I have snakes in here."

"What gave them that idea?"

"I did. I used to keep snakes, but they bored me. No conversation. And when they hissed, I thought of music critics."

"That was some far-out music," I said. "How

come I've never heard you play before?"

"I play exclusively for the one tasteful and intelligent audience to be found in this part of the world," Lenny said.

"Meaning yourself?"

"You got it, sport."

I sat down at the chair I kept near my easel in Lenny's room. Without thinking much about it, I clipped the drawing of my science-fiction castle to the stand. Lenny took off his headphones and came over to look at it.

"Gaudy," he said.

"Thanks a lot," I said elaborately. "I like your compositions on the synthesizer, too."

"No, no," Lenny said hurriedly, "I don't mean your work is gaudy. I was speaking of *Gaudi*. The Spanish architect and artist."

"Never heard of him," I admitted.

"I envy you," Lenny said. "I wish I could see his work for the first time. It's an emotional experience." He turned and began rummaging through the debris in his closet. "Now where...oh yeah, here it is!" He handed me a book titled *Art Nouveau.*

"Look in the chapter titled 'Spain,'" he urged. He rummaged around in the debris and found a pair of disreputable jockey shorts. While he put them on, I turned to the page indicated and took in my breath sharply. There it was! My science-fiction "castle" was a real building!

But it wasn't listed in the book as a castle of

any sort. It was a complete, planned apartment complex designed by Gaudi. It had provisions for shops, stalls, a plaza, a center for performing arts, and windows everywhere to let in the light. And all of it was done in exactly the style of my fantasy drawing!

I know you might not think that too much of an original concept. Any planned community or building has all the things I mentioned. Except that Gaudi designed all this in the early 1900s!

"Keep the book," Lenny said.

"Gee, are you sure?" I asked. It was a very expensive-looking book.

"Absolutely sure. You keep forgetting, Freddie. Once I've read a book, it's indelibly stamped in my memory. My sticky mind. That's why I recognized the style of your drawing. Are you sure you've never seen any of Gaudi's work? Anywhere?"

"Not that I know of." I hesitated, then it came back to me. "Wait a minute," I said, "I have seen something like it, but somehow not like it at all. The Watts Towers."

"Gotcha!" Lenny cried like Sherlock Holmes, ferreting out an elusive clue. "Rodia, who designed and built the towers, was a primitive, but his architectural sense was based on anatomy, same as Gaudi's was. That's the influence. How atypically Southern California!"

I guess I should explain. In Watts, which is the black ghetto in Los Angeles, they have these strange structures called the Watts Towers. They were built by a semi-literate immigrant to the United States named Simon Rodia. He built the whole elaborate structure himself. The towers are made of concrete, scrap, junk, and who knows what. They're decorated with bits of broken porcelain, coffee cups, plates, and broken bottles, any kind of scrap glass that will pick up and reflect light.

The towers are something of a tourist attraction, though not that many guide-book-and-camera tourists visit Watts. What knocks everyone out about Rodia's towers is that the man didn't have one bit of architectural training. The towers soar as high as 100 feet, and they're structurally sound. They've weathered a couple of earthquakes, the summer heat, and winter rains of Los Angeles. For years and years.

Only lately are they becoming fragile. But even that wasn't Rodia's fault. The smog in the air of L.A. forms an acid with the seasonal rains. That acid is consuming the concrete he used. The towers are becoming dangerous structures now. But only because of our atmosphere, not through any fault of the builder.

"But I only saw those towers once. When I was about five," I protested. "My dad took me there."

"Childhood impressions are more profound than most people realize," Lenny said. "I have no doubt that the towers were your starting point, though. Interesting."

"You sound like Mr. Spock," I said.

"I find the comparison congruent, if not accurate," Lenny said, doing an excellent Leonard Nimoy takeoff.

"Except for one thing," I said. "I can't recall ever seeing Mr. Spock in his jockey shorts."

Lenny looked down at himself and grinned. "Sorry, I wasn't expecting company," he smiled. "I would have worn a black tie, as well as my underwear."

I laughed and said, "How about a top hat, black tie, and jockey shorts, for formal concerts?"

"The very thing!" Lenny chortled. "I can see my debut at the L.A. Music Center." He went into an announcer-type voice and intoned: "Now the houselights dim, and the composer walks on stage to his own composition, 'Ode to an Athletic Supporter.' Mr. Rosenfeld checks the heating pad on his piano bench; sits down at the keyboard..." Lenny went through the motions and sat at the synthesizer. "He nods to the conductor..." Lenny nodded at an imaginary conductor, and then began to play.

This time it wasn't the far-out stuff, but churchy music, sort of. I'd never heard Lenny's setup in full volume. The speakers began belching forth great waves of sound. When Lenny hit some of the bass notes, I could almost feel the foundations of Horrid House shaking.

He finally finished the piece. I couldn't help myself. I applauded.

"You like Bach, then," Lenny said, after taking a mock bow.

"Was that Bach?"

"It's as Bach as you can get," Lenny said. "The Toccata and Fugue in D Minor. Come on, you've heard that before."

"It seemed familiar in places," I admitted.

"I can place it for you," Lenny said. He put the back of his hand to his forehead and spoke in a "Great Karnak" voice. "The toccata and fugue is what James Mason as Captain Nemo played on the organ in Disney's *Twenty Thousand Leagues Under the Sea*. Vinnie Price played it in the *Abominable Dr. Phibes*, and in the silent version of the *Phantom of the Opera*, it's the piece the house organist plays when Mary Philbin tears the mask off Lon Chaney, Sr. Got the piece now?"

"I saw *Twenty Thousand Leagues*, Lenny. You're right! That's where I heard it."

"I'm seldom wrong," Lenny admitted modestly. "But tell me, why are you haunting Horrid House like the Ghost of Thanksgiving Past?"

"You don't remember everything, Lenny," I said softly. "I have no place to go. No one to spend the holiday with. My folks..."

"My great memory," said Lenny grinning sheepishly. "But I assumed that you'd have some sort of cousin, friend, or relative you'd be with. I thought I was all alone except for Dong, downstairs."

"I'm surprised to find *you* here," I said. "I thought you might be..."

"Sharing the groaning board with Harry?" Lenny sneered. "An interesting idea. If you could find him. He's probably off to Puerto Vallarta with his latest starling, or starlet...whatever you want to call them. It doesn't matter what you call them. They all look alike: blond, great bods, and boobs. Harry's not that imaginative."

"Well, I guess we've got each other, Lenny."

"What a thrill," he said.

"Wait a minute," I said. "I've got an idea. Why don't we go to my house in Santa Amelia? We can get a turkey and all..."

"Can you cook?" Lenny asked.

"Not really," I admitted. "I know how to make some Mexican dishes, but that's about all. Except for TV dinners. I'm great with those."

"Hardly a holiday feast. Mexican dishes you say?"

"Uh-huh."

"How about some turkey tacos?" he said, and began singing an old Latin tune called "Tico-Tico." Except he sang "Turkey Taco" instead of "Tico-Tico." We both broke up over that one.

After we stopped being silly, Lenny got dressed, and for him, it was pretty formal. He put on clean jeans and a clean work shirt. As a major concession to the holiday, he didn't wear his rubber-tire sandals. He found a battered pair of sneakers in his closet and put those on. In a few minutes, we were headed for Santa Amelia in my Corvette.

"You know, I've never been to this part of the country," Lenny said as we turned into my street. "One just doesn't go to Orange County. Except under duress."

"Well, it ain't much, bro," I said, "but it's where I come from." We pulled up in front of my folks' house.

The house was dark except for a light coming from my room. I knew it had to be Mrs. Fernandez. I checked my watch. It was half past nine at night. Dinner at Mrs. Fernandez's daughter's house would have been long over. And tomorrow being a working day for most people in the neighborhood, some houses were already dark for the night.

I went up to the porch and was about to use my house key, when I stopped. "What's wrong?" Lenny asked.

"I oughta ring the bell," I said.

"Why? It's your house, isn't it?"

"Yeah, it is. But I didn't call Mrs. Fernandez to say we were coming. She might think someone was breaking in. And call the cops. I better knock and ring the bell."

"Take no chances, Freddie. I don't fancy spending Thanksgiving in the Santa Amelia slam for house-breaking."

I rang the bell and began knocking at the door. In a few moments, the hall and porch lights went on. Mrs. Fernandez's face appeared for a second behind the curtain in the glass inset of the front door.

If I expected a big welcome from her, I was way off base.

"Go away," she said from behind the closed door. "Nobody home. Nobody home."

"Talking mice?" Lenny volunteered.

"Don't be smart," I said. Then to Mrs. Fernandez, through the door, I said, *"Señora Fernandez. Es yo. Alfredo. ¿No me conece?"* Which means, it's me, Freddie. Don't you know me? Her face appeared at the corner of the glass inset again.

"Don't make jokes, señor," she said, in Spanish. "Freddie is away at school. I get letters from him. I spoke to him on the phone last Sunday. Now, what do you want here? And who are you?"

"Honest. It's me!" I said again in Spanish, then in English.

The door opened a crack, with the inner safety chain in place. Then it closed and opened full. Mrs. Fernandez was standing there in a nightgown and bathrobe. She opened her arms wide and smiled.

"Freddie! Forgive me. I didn't know you! What happened to you? You look like an Anglo! I wasn't going to let you in..."

She stopped when she saw Lenny in the porch light. Obviously Lenny could give anyone pause. Mrs. Fernandez is under five feet tall. And Lenny is six-four. He must have looked like the Jolly White Giant to her.

112

"*Ay Diós!*" she exclaimed. "*Es un gípi!*" The word was close enough for Lenny to recognize. She was calling him a hippie. Lenny gave a mock bow and said, "*Señor* Gípi, at your service, madame."

Mrs. Fernandez stood stock still for a second, then burst out laughing. She stopped then, suddenly, a look of embarrassment coming across her face.

"What's the matter with me?" she asked rhetorically. "I keep you standing out here on the porch. Come in, come in!" She led the way to the kitchen. We followed.

I ought to explain that, too. When you have company in my part of Santa Amelia, you take them into the *sala*, the parlor. But if it's family, the room is the kitchen. The kitchen is the center of any working-class Latino household. In a few seconds, we were seated around Mom's big oak table in the kitchen, and a pot of strong coffee was on the stove.

"Did you have dinner?" Mrs. Fernandez asked.

"Not yet," I admitted.

"*Ay que lástima.* What a shame," she said. "To think that my best friend's son had no Thanksgiving dinner." She began rummaging through the fridge. "I have some leftovers that my daughter gave me to take home. Could you eat a hot turkey sandwich?"

"I could eat this table," Lenny volunteered.

"What do I call you?" Mrs. Fernandez said pointedly to Lenny. "Your name isn't Gípi. Even if

113

you *look* like one," she added with a sniff.

Lenny laughed and said to me, "You now see the difference between Beverly Hills and Santa Amelia. I can be served at Le Bistro dressed like this, but Santa Amelia can't be snowed by implied money. You dress, or you don't eat!"

"*Pobrecito*," said Mrs. Fernandaz, her hand flying to her mouth. "I meant nothing. I didn't know you had no other clothes. Forgive me, uh..."

"*Leonardo, señora*," Lenny said. "*Leonardo Rosenfeld, me gusto mucho de encontrarse. Su servidor, señora.*"

I sat at the table, with my jaw hanging low enough to kick. Lenny's choice of words and his accent were flawless! Mrs. Fernandez was beaming at him. He was obviously not a Latino, but he was speaking Spanish, and well. That means a lot to old folks, you know. You don't have to speak Spanish well. Just the idea that you would do them the courtesy of trying is enough.

"Where did you pick that up?" I said to Lenny after the reciprocal niceties of a Spanish introduction were done with.

"Spain," Lenny smiled. "Harry was making an opus called *Go Get 'Em Yanks!* in Spain. It was a World War II, hairy-chest copy of *Dirty Dozen*.

"You can't afford all the extras you need in a flick if you shoot in the States. They shoot in Spain or Yugoslavia. We were there for a year, shooting the film. My mother was alive then, and she put me in

114

a good boarding school in Barcelona. That s how I knew Gaudi. His work is all over Barcelona."

Mrs. Fernandez served us a couple of creditable hot turkey sandwiches. I know she was dying to hear all my news, but in true old-fashioned style, she didn't sit down with us. It didn't have to do with women's rights. It had to do with me being her landlord.

I felt the subtle distance almost immediately. True, at first when she recognized me, she gave me a big hug, *un abrazo*. But after that, she got formal. It hurt me a bit, too.

This woman had changed my diapers when I was a baby. She was ten years older than my mom. Sort of like someone's aunt that always seems to be living with the family. Now, she kept her distance. It had to be my new clothes and haircut. The only comment she made to me was in Spanish, and quite fast.

"Why are you sitting there?" she almost whispered as she served us. "Sit where you belong! You have a guest!"

It took a second to sink in. We have five chairs around the kitchen table. One for each member of what used to be my family. One of the chairs is what you'd call a captain's chair, I guess. It has arms; the others don't. It was my father's chair. Mrs. Fernandez was telling me that *I* was the head of the household now. I knew she was right, but somehow, I couldn't bring myself to sit in Dad's chair. Maybe some other time. But not on a holiday.

Mrs. Fernandez excused herself, saying that she'd miss her favorite show on TV. She watches SIN a lot. No, it's not like that. It's S.I.N. actually. Stands for Spanish International Network. They're the outfit that shows all the flicks and variety shows in Spanish on UHF television.

"Well, my friend," Lenny said, wiping his mouth with the back of his hand, ignoring the paper napkins Mrs. Fernandez had set out, "that was just the ticket for a Thanksgiving meal at home." He saw the look on my face and added, "Say, what's wrong, pal? You look like someone shot Santa Claus."

I explained to him the feeling I got from Mrs. Fernandez. And about my dad's chair at the table. He was suddenly all concern.

"You know, I must be some sort of callous clot," Lenny said. "I was so depressed about spending the holiday alone, I never thought about you. Wrapped up in my self-pity. I've spent every holiday alone since my mother died, you know.

"Over the years, I've ignored holidays. Then, you invite me to your home to cheer me up. And you did cheer me, Freddie. But I never thought about what it's cost you, emotionally. Coming back to an empty home, so soon after your family...uh..."

"Died," I put in. "It's okay to say it out loud, Lenny. I had to come to terms with it. Yeah, I keep getting the feeling that any minute now, they'll all show up laughing, ready for turkey dinner. But in

116

my heart, I know they won't...not ever. I can live with it. I have to."

"Well, you don't have to do it here," Lenny said. "Too many sad memories in this house. Come on. We're leaving!"

"Where to?"

"Well, I can't reciprocate and take you to my house. Even with Harry away, that mausoleum depresses me. Let me make a phone call, okay?"

"Sure. It's on the wall, behind you."

Lenny got on the phone and dialed a direct number. "Hello," he said into the phone. "Give me front desk, please...Hello? Front desk? This is Leonard Rosenfeld...Yes, that's right, Harry's son." Lenny put a hand over the mouthpiece and said to me, "You don't know how it galls me to be identified that way." Then: "Yes, yes...fine. Which bungalow is open? No. That won't do...ah, you do? Well, Harry's out of town. I'll be using it. Arrive in...an hour and a half...yes...same to you; happy Thanksgiving. G'bye."

Lenny turned to me with a huge smile and said, "There you go, my dear Flores. We will spend the balance of the holiday weekend at the Beverly Hilton. Harry keeps a bungalow there for visiting VIPs from back East. Also for visits from his starlets. But Harry is in Puerto Vallarta. And while the rat's away, us cats will play!"

Which is just what we did. We arrived at the hour designated and spent the rest of the weekend

117

in what Lenny called "sybaritic splendor."

He called up some of his Hollywood acquaintances and we partied for a while that night. We even had a small rock combo to play for us!

I don't know what the Hollywood crowd thought of their hosts. Lenny and I were the only ones at the party who didn't smoke or drink. Me, because I don't. Lenny because he swore off it when he had his accident. But I promise you, like the old joke goes: you don't have to smoke and drink to have a good time.

The next few nights, through Lenny and his magic telephone, we got tickets to shows and sporting events. By the time Monday came around, I was ready to go back to Valverde. If only for some rest. But as it turned out, there wasn't much rest to be found at VV.

When the grades for mid-term exams were posted, I got a very happy surprise. I not only passed math, but overall, I was one of the top ten students in my class!

I'd been awfully worried. It seemed that in each class except for art, all the other kids knew the answers. Or they seemed to, during question-and-answer periods. But as Lenny had pointed out, most of the kids were just talking a good fight. They'd ask proper, penetrating, and perceptive questions in class. But they were all jiving, it seems. That kind of classroom action is a ploy to make the teacher think you know the work.

But when the grades came down, it was *Flores, A.* who got the A's and one B-plus. Math, of course. I was riding high and hurried back to share my news with Lenny. On account of my grades were higher than a certain *Castillo, R.* My mind was filled with a thousand thoughts when I went upstairs to Room 208.

The door was open when I got there, and the room was crowded. There was Snotty Roddie, Mrs. Hargrove, Mr. Cassidy, the Administrative Assistant to the Dean, Dean Schuler, and a uniformed school security guard.

The mattress on my bed was turned back. Folded over, really. I began to say: "Who? What?" and all the things you say when you're completely taken by surprise. Then I saw it.

You don't have to smoke the stuff to know what it looks like. Not in my neighborhood, anyway. Lying on the box spring were a dozen one-ounce Ziploc bags of marijuana!

10

As soon as I saw those bags spread out on the top of my box spring, I knew what had happened. I'd been set up by Snotty Roddie. I hadn't taken his warning seriously enough. He'd gotten back at me all right. With bells on!

"Come in, Alfredo," said Dean Schuler in a chilly tone. "We don't wish to have this affair made public knowledge."

I didn't say anything but just went into the room. I had to almost laugh out loud at what Dean Schuler said, though. I was willing to bet that Snotty Roddie had the news all over the campus. Well before it happened. After all, he had set the whole thing up. I knew that for sure.

And logically, who would have more reason and chance to do it? I could piece it together, easy. All Roddie had to do was go home over the holiday and pick up as much weed as he wanted. San Martin is famous for the marijuana they grow down there. He'd have no trouble taking it through customs, either. A customs official wouldn't search the son of a head of state. Especially one of the few Central American states still on good terms with the United States.

After that, it would be a simple matter to plant the stuff under my mattress. I was hardly ever in the room. I did all my studying down the hall, in Lenny's room.

I looked at Roddie. He was impassive about it, to judge from the look on his face. You slimy creep, I thought. Do you really think I don't know you're behind this?

"This is a very serious matter, Alfredo," Dean Schuler was saying. "You are fortunate in a sense that this has happened here at Valverde. We do not call the authorities over such affairs. Perhaps, in our desire to protect the reputation of Valverde, we may allow some offenses to go unpunished. Naturally, you will resign from the academy, and we will notify either your guardian or the police."

How neat and nice, I thought. A real kangaroo court. Here's the stuff, kid. You're guilty. Get out and we won't sic The Man on you.

"Have you heard a word I have said, young

man?" Dean Schuler asked. "This is very grave."

"He's probably doped to the eyelids," volunteered the rent-a-cop. And to me, he said, "Do you know what's going on, kid? Are you loaded?"

I ignored the rent-a-cop. He probably thought he was being hip, talking in street rap to me. I went over to the stash and picked up one of the bags. I turned to the happy little group that was gathered to see me get the ax.

I thought of saying a million things. I thought of telling all present that Snotty Roddie had been on my case since Registration Week. I thought of telling them just how he could have set me up. I thought of blowing the whistle on him and his porno tapes for the video cassette player.

But I knew that if Roddie had set me up so neatly, he would have gotten all that filthy stuff out of the room. Probably handed them off to one of his goons in the Caddy limo outside the gates.

Most of all, I realized how cute Roddie had been. No one even knew of the bad blood between us. He'd been careful to dump on me only when there was no one around. Sure, Lenny knew. He had eavesdropped. But that doesn't count. In the end, it came down to my word against Roddie's. Some contest.

Who was going to take the word of Alfredo Flores, late of Santa Amelia and low riders fame, against the word of Roderigo Alondra y Castillo? He was a millionaire, A student, athlete, and future ruler of the Independent Republic of San Martin. I'd been done for. So neatly that I didn't stand a prayer.

I dropped the bag of weed back onto the bed. Then I turned to Dean Schuler and asked: "Is this it? I get no hearing, no trial, no nothing?"

He looked a bit uncomfortable for a second. Then as stiff as ever he said, "Of course, if you desire a hearing, you may have one. You may have witnesses to testify as to your character. Perhaps some mitigation or explanation could be tendered..."

Wow. All he could think of was me pleading to stay on at VV. Bring in some folks who would say what a swell guy I am. It was obvious that Schuler never once doubted my guilt! I mentally shrugged my shoulders. No point in prolonging the farce.

"I'll say this once," I said, trying to control my rage at the setup. "I don't use marijuana. I never have. I don't smoke cigarettes, or anything else. I take aspirin when I have a headache and Contac pills when I have a cold. That is the sum total of all my experience with drugs. And all of you are condemning me on some..." I looked right at Snotty Roddie when I said this "...anonymous tipster, full of school spirit." Roddie didn't so much as flinch or avoid my eyes. He returned my gaze with a stare of mixed contempt and hatred. "But I can see that doesn't mean anything to you," I continued. "You have your minds made up. So do I. Goodbye."

I didn't say any more. I turned and walked out of the room. I was on my way out, when I heard

Lenny come clattering down the stairs after me.

"Freddie, wait!" he said.

I turned to see him, halfway down the stairs. He stopped in midstep. His eyes met mine for a long second. I guess he read it on my face. Nothing he could say, or do, would change anything. He gave me a sad look, than forced his features into his normal smile. He came over to where I was standing and put his arms around me in a traditional *abrazo*.

"*Adiós, amigo*," he said. "It's not over. I won't let them do this to you."

"You don't understand, Lenny," I said flatly. "It's over. You've been a good guy. I'll stay in touch." Then I went out the door and around the house to the parking lot.

I sat in the car without starting it up. I realized that I had walked out without my toothbrush, any clothes, or my personal stuff. Then I knew that anything I had left behind could be replaced for money. And I had all I needed.

I twisted the starter key and gunned the engine of the Corvette into growling life. It made a satisfying sound. I laid rubber all over the parking lot and was just shifting into third gear as I approached the security gate at the end of Campus Drive.

I didn't stop until I pulled up in front of my folks' house in Santa Amelia. I put the 'Vette inside the garage, so no one would know I was in the house.

Mrs. Fernandez wasn't in. I was glad. I didn't want to talk to anyone or see anyone. My anger was cooling a bit now. More than anything else, I wanted a chance to think.

I went into my old room and got out of my Anglo masquerade costume. I put on my chinos, sneakers, and plaid shirt. It's the *barrio* uniform. To Anglos, it makes you anonymous. You look like any other Chicano kid on the street. And that's exactly what I wanted to look like.

I checked the cash I had. Twenty-odd bucks. Not enough for what I wanted to do. I had to hit the bank first. I still hadn't cashed my monthly allowance check from Callen: five hundred bucks. I was on my way out when I ran into Mrs. Fernandez, at the door with a sack of groceries.

"'Fredo!" she cried. "You look like yourself again! But what are you doing here? I thought..."

"*Lo siento*," I said, "I'm sorry. I don't have time to talk. I quit that school. Seems I'm not the kind they want there."

Mrs. Fernandez gave me a look that bespoke immediate understanding and a lifetime of knowing there were places neither of us would ever be welcome. "*Yo entiendo*, Freddie. I understand," she said.

For the first time since I had gone off to Valverde, I heard someone say to me that they understood and knew that they *did*. I didn't say another word. I hugged her and gave her a small kiss on the cheek. Then I opened the garage and got the car out. As I drove away from the house, Mrs. Fernandez was still on the porch, watching me go. The last I saw

125

was from my rear-view mirror. She slowly put her hand to the cheek I had kissed.

The Sierra Mountains are quite close to Santa Amelia. You drive about two hours and you start to hit desert. Another hour and a half, it's what they call high desert. From there, you can see the mountains clearly. The roads run straight as a string and if there's not too much traffic, you can really clip along.

On account of visibility there, it's impossible for a cop to hide behind anything for a speed trap. I opened up the 'Vette and turned on my tape deck. I drove steadily until I came to the High Sierras. I got as far as Mammoth when I was stopped by a cop.

Oh, I wasn't speeding or anything. I'd cooled off enough by then. This cop stopped me inside of the town limits. Why? You got to be kidding! He wanted to know what the Mex kid in *barrio* uniform was doing driving a car like mine.

I was too sick inside to cause a fuss. I just showed him my license and registration and my proof of ownership of the car. Oh, wow, I thought. Isn't there anyplace in the world where I won't get rousted because of who I am? What I look like?

It was the tail end of autumn in the mountains. Too early for snow and the skiers. I had no trouble getting a room at a nice place. I told the desk that I didn't want to be disturbed, no matter what. What a gag. No one knew me or cared.

I stayed up in the mountains for ten days. I didn't see anyone or talk to anyone. Unless you count some storekeepers. I bought a fleece-lined jacket for the cold night air and some toilet gear. At the restaurants where I ate, I ate alone.

The place I stayed was Bear Lodge. It had one central building and a number of cabins around it. I rented one of the cabins. It was on a lake. There was a little island, just off the lakeshore, that you could get to by a footbridge. Once on the little island, you could sit on some benches made of stones from the area. Off in the distance, through the clean, clear mountain air, you could see a waterfall. One day, I hiked up the foot trail and sat at the edge, looking down on the world.

Mostly, I thought and thought hard. I had to work out in my mind what had happened to me. And why. Where I had gone wrong. It was the first time since my folks had died that I'd done that. I wished with all my heart that Dad was alive. To talk to.

Not that we talked all that much when Dad was alive. He was always bushed from working at the plastics factory when he came home. And I guess you think that your parents will always be there. I'm sure that Dad had meant to have long talks with me, someday. But sudden death took that someday away.

I had nobody's counsel but my own. On the tenth day, I came to a decision. I checked out of the lodge and headed back to Santa Amelia.

I hadn't gone more than a hundred miles toward Los Angeles when I got stopped again. No speeding, no erratic driving. I sighed heavily as the cop approached my car.

I had my license and registration out by the time he reached me. I saw him come walking up and swallowed hard. He was unsnapping the leather strap that held his gun in the holster!

I knew *this* drill. I was careful to keep my license and registration between the two first fingers of my left hand and my other hand in plain view on the steering wheel. California cops are a nervous sort, and they tend to shoot first and ask questions later. Especially if you're a Chicano.

The cop came up and took my papers and checked them out. "You are Alfredo Flores?" he asked, looking from me to the picture on my license. I was about to give him a wise-ass answer. Then I realized that with my new haircut and White Stag fleece-lined ski jacket, I didn't look much like the old picture on my license.

"Yes, I'm Flores," I said wearily, "and this is my car, if you check the registration. I'm not speeding or drinking. I just want to get home to Santa Amelia. That's in Orange County."

"Oh, I know where it is, Mr. Flores," said the cop. I did a take. He had called me *Mister*! "You've had a number of people very concerned for you, Mr. Flores," the cop went on.

"How's that?" I asked.

"Haven't you seen a paper or turned on the TV or radio?" the cop asked.

"No," I admitted. "I've been up in the mountains, having some quiet time. They didn't have a TV. And I didn't read the papers."

"You should have, Mr. Flores," he said. "There's been a statewide search going on for you. The past five days. Back in Orange County, they think you may have been kidnapped."

I was stunned. Hadn't anyone talked to Mrs. Fernandez? She had seen me leave under my own power. True, I hadn't told her where I was headed. How could I? I didn't know myself!

"I think I better make some phone calls," I said.

"I think so, too," the cop said. "I'll have to radio in a call that you've been found."

"I was never lost," I protested.

"Don't say that, please Mr. Flores," the cop said. "Your guardian has a ten-thousand-dollar reward offered for your whereabouts. It's close to Christmas, and it sure would help things around my house, sir."

In a flash, I knew where all the swell treatment was coming from. The cop didn't see me as a lost person. Just as a ten-thousand-dollar bill attached to a kid. What the hell, I thought. Let him get off on his reward. "Anything you want to do is okay with me," I said.

The cop broke into a big grin and hotfooted it for his car radio. Halfway there, he stopped and turned around. I knew what was on his mind. I stuck my head out the window and hollered, "It's okay. I'm not going anywhere!" Satisfied that his Christmas money wasn't going to run away, he ran to the car and began calling in for his reward.

I went to Bishop, the nearest town, and called John Callen.

"Freddie, where are you?" he sputtered. "We've had the Highway Patrol, the FBI..."

"Call them off," I said. "I'm okay. I wasn't even lost. I had to get away for a while. Do some thinking. I'm on my way back now."

"We must have a long talk, Freddie," Callen began.

"In due time, in due time," I said. "Right now, I want to get home. I have a lot of things to do. People to see."

"Very well, Freddie. I understand," Callen replied.

"Do you?" I asked. "I wouldn't be too sure." Then I hung up.

When I got back to my folks' house in Santa Amelia there were two cars in the driveway. One, I recognized. It was Callen's Lincoln town car. The other, a Porsche, I'd never seen before.

When I walked into the living room, it was like a party waiting to happen. Callen was there, seated in my dad's lounger. Lenny Rosenfeld sat on the couch, nearby. I wondered if he'd broken his vow not to drive again. Was it his Porsche in the driveway?

Just then, Nat Simpson came into the room from

the kitchen. She saw me, let out a squeal, and threw a full bearhug around my neck.

"Freddie, where have you been?" she asked. "We've all been worried sick!"

Before I got a chance to answer, she laid a big welcome-home kiss on me. When I looked up, I saw Lenny and Callen busy trying to look nonchalant. Callen cleared his throat.

"We have to talk, Freddie," he said.

"Talk away," I said. "We're all friends here."

"It's about this business at Valverde," Callen said.

"Forget it," I said. "It's all over. I've had some time to think...that's what I went away for...and I'm not going back there. I never did belong there."

Callen shifted in his chair. "Then your being totally exonerated doesn't mean anything?" he asked. He reached into his jacket pocket and took out a letter. "Take a look at this," he said.

It was on Valverde stationery, and it was from Dean Schuler. I read the first few paragraphs, then started to laugh. It read, in part:

> Through John Callen, and certain other sources at Valverde, we have discovered a serious injustice has been done to you. In view of this new information, we feel an apology is due. We should like to beg your pardon, and let you know that you would be most welcome to return to Valverde Academy at any time...

The letter went on to say that Schuler had acted in good faith, on what he thought was fact. He never did name the "certain other sources." But one thing was sure. I was in the clear. The truth had come out after all. But who had done it? Who had come forward?

Just then, I saw something on the porch, outside the *sala* window. There was this Anglo, looking in the window. He had a camera, and he was taking my picture! "What's going on?" I cried.

"Reporters," Callen said. "You forget you're an important person, Freddie. When someone worth millions disappears for over a week, it's news. They're all dying to know why you left Valverde, then vanished." Callen smiled thinly. "And I think that Schuler is dying right now, too. He's afraid you'll tell the press."

"He doesn't have to worry," I said. "I'd just as soon forget the whole thing happened." Then I stopped talking. If I had been a cartoon character, a little light bulb would have appeared over my head. That's why Callen got the letter of apology. Justice didn't matter. Only keeping Valverde's reputation clean. I told Callen what I thought.

"You're probably right, Freddie," he said. "But you can't blame the man. The whole school could be hurt badly."

"And what about me?" I asked. "He didn't care a fat rat's ass about justice when I was on the wrong end of it. Now that the truth can hurt him, he wants to bury it."

"It's not a bad school, Freddie," Callen said. "And they have turned out some fine students. Don't get me wrong now," he said, holding up a hand. "I think Schuler ought to be roasted over a slow fire. If you're going to let the matter drop, as you say, don't let him know right away. Let him sweat a bit. Maybe he won't be so fast to judge, next time. If there *is* a next time. That's up to you."

I thought about Valverde, and Schuler. Sure, there were some stiffs there. But there were also really nice people, like Mr. Schwartzberg and Mrs. Hargrove. And I *had* met Natalie and Lenny there. I smiled at the idea of Schuler turning on the barbecue machine at Lara's Drive-In.

"I'll call him first thing tomorrow," I told Callen. "And without any revenge, or comebacks. None of it matters anymore...not even Roddie." Callen looked relieved.

"I think that's a wise decision, Freddie," he said. "You could, of course, sue. And I wouldn't enjoy destroying a good school because one man made a bad decision."

"Well, if that's all over," Lenny said with a grin, "let's party!"

=11=

WE ALL STARTED TO TALK AT THE SAME time...words falling out like popcorn from a machine. Lenny went into his impression of Dean Schuler. Natalie and I laughed till our sides hurt. Then abruptly, Callen cleared his throat.

"If I may, I'd like to say a few words," he said.

"Speak, o oracle of the legal profession," Lenny said. "We await with bait on our breaths." He belched softly behind his hand. "Must have been the anchovies on the pizza I had for lunch."

"If you don't mind, Mr. Rosenfeld," Callen said, "I wish to speak to Freddie in private. If that's all right with you, Freddie."

"Sure," I said. "Come on, we'll go into the kitchen."

I led the way. Callen sat down at the table. Before I sat down, I did something I'd never done before. I went to the cupboard over the fridge, where I knew Dad had always kept a bottle of Canadian Club. I took it down and poured a shot for Callen in a small Kraft cheese jar glass. Then I sat down in the captain's chair at the head of the table. My chair. I had a few things to say to Callen. I was glad he wanted to talk.

"I know you're curious about what happened after you left," he said. "I heard about the railroad job they did on you. Your friend Rosenfeld called and told me. But by the time I'd gotten to your house here, you'd left." I nodded.

"Your Mrs. Fernandez was somehow convinced that you were on the run from the authorities. She wouldn't say a word to anyone about you. Other than you had left in your car." Good for her! I thought.

"But when you didn't surface for five days, we began to fear that you'd met with foul play. I called the authorities. I offered a reward..."

"I know," I said. "There's a cop in Bishop who's richer by ten grand tonight. You gave him a very merry Christmas. Or did you offer *my* money for the reward?"

Callen blinked. "You know, it never occurred to me whose money I was offering. I was concerned only with your safe return." I let that one slide.

"Listen, Mr. Callen," I said. "I did some heavy

thinking while I was away. About what's happened to me and why. To tell you the truth, you don't come off too well."

"How do you mean?"

"You knew very well what Valverde was like. Yet you let me go there without even trying to wise me up a tiny bit."

"You'll recall that it was *you* who brought up wanting to pursue your education, not I," Callen said.

"True enough," I admitted. "But it was *you* who thought of beautiful Valverde Academy."

"I had the connections through Schuler. It's a good school," Callen said. "You make of it what you will."

"Swell," I said. "And you couldn't let me know that looking like what I did back then, I'd go over like a leper in a steam bath? You clammed up. You could have told me when I bought that car that they'd think it was flashy and in poor taste at VV."

"You never asked me," Callen countered. "I heard about the scene you made at Grober's Chevrolet. You bludgeoned that car salesman with your money and influence. A poor use of money and a worse use of the power implicit in having it."

Callen took a sip of whiskey. He smiled. "I used to drink Canadian Club," he said. "But as I grew wealthier, I began to drink scotch. I think I just realized I never did like scotch. I haven't enjoyed a drink of whiskey in years!"

"You were saying?" I demanded.

"I suppose I could have told you more about Valverde and its overprivileged student body. But you had no basis of comparison by which to judge it."

"So you just threw me in the ocean to teach me how to swim, eh? And didn't tell me there were sharks."

"I had great faith in your ability to survive, Freddie. I knew that if it got rough, you wouldn't complain; you'd work it out somehow."

"Gee, thanks a lot," I said. "And now that I've shown I can swim faster than the sharks, it's all peachy keen, huh? You now welcome me with open arms, and say, 'Gee, Freddie. You passed my personal test of character, and now I will admit you into the inner circles. You can even call me Jack, if you want.' Is that it?"

"Something like that," Callen said. "I'd hoped you would understand."

"I understand more than you think I do," I said, getting angry.

But I cooled myself. I had done a lot of thinking about this minute with Callen. I stood up and leaned halfway across the table until my face was inches from his.

"How dare you play God with my life?" I demanded. "What ever made you think you had the right to test me and my character? You're no blood of mine. Not my parent. Not my anything but an account keeper until I'm twenty-one! And as far as that goes, I can have my guardian changed!"

Callen looked at me without flinching. He said quietly, "Sit down, young man. You don't intimidate me. Yes, there is truth in your argument. Yes, I played God. But in the process, I think I did you more good than harm. You were a green-as-grass, insular, low-income Latino kid. You had no more idea of the fortune left you than a babe in the woods. You showed that by abusing your authority the first time you had a chance.

"You were rough as a cob, Freddie," he said. "I knew what you'd run into at Valverde. And as I say, I had faith in you. If you'll assess what has happened, you'd see it too.

"What's come to pass, really? You have dropped out of Valverde without prejudice or cloud over your name. And ultimately, what does Valverde matter? You didn't want to go there to begin with. Or Stanford, either. You were filled with hate and distrust after you'd lost your family, boy."

"Don't call me boy!" I snapped.

"Don't act like one!" he came back savagely. "As I was saying, Valverde doesn't matter. What does matter is that you've become aware of the world outside the *barrio*. You learned it harshly and abruptly.

"But hard-learned lessons are the ones that stay with you through life. No, I don't regret what I did for a second. You're going to get on in life, Freddie, and get on just fine. If you don't like me for what

I did, that's unfortunate. I promise you, I won't lose a single night's sleep over it."

"I'd bet on that," I put in.

"You can do what you like, Freddie," said Callen. "You don't have to like me. As you pointed out, I am neither kin nor kith to you. But I am a man of a certain reputation for honesty and integrity. You won't find a better administrator or a more zealous guardian. I'm the best sort, son. I'll leave you be to make your own mistakes. I'll also leave you free to pay for them. I know now, that I won't be nursing some *nouveau riche* snotty kid through the remainder of his adolescence.

"But just what is it you want?" Callen asked. "You have more than most men could wish for. It doesn't seem to have made you happy."

"I'm not sure, myself," I admitted. "I think it's something out of a book I read. I was only ten. It was a kid's book. About this kid who wakes up one morning, and finds out he's a dog."

"I beg your pardon?" Callen said. "Did you say a dog?"

"Yeah. You know. Like, bow-wow? Anyway, the kid goes nearly nuts. He knows that inside, he's still a kid. But all people can see is a mutt dog."

"Interesting concept," Callen said.

"I only read the book because of the cover illustration," I said. "It showed a dog in pajamas, trying to shave. That, and it was written by a Latino... in English.

"There was this poem in the book...or maybe it was a song. But I can still remember the name of it: 'The Me Inside of Me.' Maybe that's what I'm looking for...someplace where they can see the me inside of me. Not a Chicano with an Anglo haircut and clothes. A guy who doesn't fit anyplace. I want them to see Freddie Flores, with no labels."

"That's a tall order, Freddie," Callen said. "We live in a world of labels and instant identification. I wish you luck in finding that place." He got up from his chair.

"I have to go now," he said. "My family expected me for dinner hours ago. I won't offer you friendship, Freddie. I don't think you want or expect that from me. I'm glad. Most of my friends are my own age. Do what you want about changing my status as your guardian. I'll help out and draw up the papers, once you've found someone else. I hope you choose properly. But then again, that's your choice. I'm confident you'll make the right one."

Callen stopped at the kitchen door and peered out. "Oh hell!" he grumbled. "They're out in back, too! Will you do me a favor and give the press a statement later? They won't give anyone any peace until you do. Goodbye, Freddie."

He was halfway out the door when I stopped him. "Mr. Callen?"

"Yes, Freddie?"

"You never did answer my question. Why did you do what you did? You already said that you don't even particularly like me."

"I said that I respect your judgment and maturity," Callen said with a funny smile. "Don't press your luck. There are few men I say that of. As to why I did it. I genuinely liked your grandfather. Wilfredo Flores was a gentleman and a professional."

Then he was gone out the door, and the flash-bulbs started popping all around him. I saw him make his way to his car, shaking his head to all questions and waving reporters and cameramen away from him. He kept his head down and walked rapidly. But with authority.

The crowd cleared in front of him. He got into the big Lincoln sedan I'd seen in the driveway and took off. I went back to the living room. I wanted to find out about some things. And only Lenny and maybe Natalie could tell me.

12

"WHERE'S MRS. FERNANDEZ?" I ASKED when I came back into the living room.

"She said she didn't want to miss 'Happy Days,'" Lenny said. "It seems Mrs. Fernandez digs the Fonz."

"It's an addiction with her," I admitted. "But she's an old lady. Staying here, she gets to see what she wants instead of what her grandchildren watch."

"I like her," Natalie said. "Half the state was searching for you, and she was silent as a tomb. She didn't understand what all the fuss was. And because there were police involved, she wouldn't speak English. Lenny spoke to her in Spanish..."

"Spanglish," Lenny corrected. "I couldn't dignify

what I speak by calling it Spanish."

"Whatever," Natalie said. "You've got some ally there, Fred."

"And right here, too," I said. "I'm dying to know what happened. When I bugged out of VV I thought it was all over. I came back, and all of a sudden, I'm a prince. I was in the dark about what Schuler was talking about. 'Certain information': What's that?"

Nat and Lenny looked at each other. "You or me first?" Nat said.

"Me first," Lenny said. "I'm a natural-born story-teller. Besides, I know more of the whole picture than you do."

"Modest to the end, eh Lenny?" I gibed.

"I see no point in false modesty," Lenny smiled. "Do you want to hear how you became a wronged hero instead of a dead duck, or don't you?"

"Speak on."

"Okay. When Snotty Roddie staged his little drama in your room, I was down the hall. I was working with my Moog synthesizer, so I didn't hear the early parts. By the time you had run out, it was too late for me to get the whole picture."

"I wasn't about to stay," I said. "Schuler had already found me guilty without a trial."

"So I figured," Lenny said. "I peeked into the room and saw the smoke laid out on your mattress. I knew something had to be done. But for once, my lightning mental processes didn't flash instantly.

143

I had to lay out a plan."

"Meanwhile, over at Brice House," Nat said, like a film narrator, "word was out. Soon as I heard about it, I knew it wasn't so. I know you don't even smoke cigarettes. It didn't occur to me to contact Lenny. Not at first. I had no idea how tight you two were."

"Understandable," Lenny commented. "When one is out with a gorgeous creature like yourself, another man would hardly be a topic of conversation. Despite how fascinating I am."

"I knew that Mr. Schwartzberg is a big fan of yours, Freddie," Nat went on. "I went to him and told him about your problems. Told him I thought you'd been framed."

"What did he say?" I asked.

"I d-d-don't b-believe it, either," said Nat, mimicking. "He went to Dean Schuler's office. He told me later that he had given you his personal endorsement. He begged Schuler to reinstate you."

I whistled softly. I know what it costs Schwartzberg to talk to anyone, let alone Schuler.

"And I," Lenny picked up, "formulated my master plan. After the dust had settled, I went to Schuler. Told him that someone had seen Roddie set you up. That he got the smoke handed to him by one of his goons in the Caddy. And that he was seen bringing the dope into Horrid House."

"No kidding?" I croaked. "What a break! I didn't know anyone cared that much about me to come forward. Who saw him do it?"

"I did," Lenny said smugly. "I saw the whole thing, Dean Schuler." he said, going into a scene "'Why didn't you tell me of this sooner, Rosenfeld?'" Lenny said, imitating Schuler's prissy speech. "I didn't know what was going on, sir," Lenny replied to himself. "'Well, that certainly lends a different cast to this matter,'" he said, as Schuler. "'We seem to have made a serious error.'"

"But Lenny," I put in. "When did you see all this?"

"I didn't," Lenny said, leaning back in his chair and lacing his fingers behind his head. "I lied."

"You lied?"

"You heard me. I told you I had a plan. I sat down and assessed the situation logically. Point A," he said, holding up a finger. "Roddie had framed you. He was lying through his teeth. But I know enough of the politics at Valverde to predict that Schuler would believe Roddie over you.

"Point B," he went on, holding up a second finger. "If Roddie's word was stronger than yours, you needed somebody with a word stronger than Snotty Roddie's."

"Namely?"

"Namely Point C: me! If Roddie was lying, I lied, too. One canceled out the other. You see, Roddie may be the son of a generalissimo, and his father may be a heavy contributor to VV. Harry, on the other hand, is a *bona fide* movie mogul. Central

American dictators come and go, but if I can believe the *Wall Street Journal*, Galactic Pictures and its subsidiaries will go on forever. My lie, ergo, was a stronger one than Snotty Roddie's."

Lenny sat back in his chair, waiting for some sort of praise, I guess. But I wasn't that happy about what I was learning.

"So, just on your say-so, Schuler reversed himself?" I asked.

"Far from it," Lenny conceded. "I had to ram it down his throat and use all the clout I had. And just in case he might have been slow to act, I called your man, Callen, and told him."

"You lied to Callen, too?" I gasped.

"Absolutely," Lenny said. "Then, when you did your vanishing act, Callen threw in the idea to Schuler that you may have done yourself harm."

"Are you nuts?" I said. "Why would I do a thing like that?"

"Well, I'm not certain that Callen threw that part in," Lenny admitted. "I just know that *I* would, in the same situation. As to you being depressed enough to do something foolish, that's not off base at all. You've had some tremendous emotional body blows dealt to you of late. Your parents, adjusting to a new school and a totally different *milieu*. And then, getting dusted off by Nefertiti here," he said, indicating Natalie.

"Oh, don't look so shocked, Freddie. She told me. She thought that maybe she was responsible in part for what happened."

I glanced over at Natalie. She shrugged eloquently. "I just didn't know, that's all," she offered.

Lenny stood up. "Well, all's well that et cetera," he said. "I believe a certain amount of celebration is in order. Treat's on me." He stopped talking when I didn't respond.

"What's wrong, good friend?" he asked. "You don't look like a man who's recently avoided the noose and gotten a medal, besides."

"It's not right, Lenny," I said. "I wasn't cleared at all. I was set up with a lie. Then I was cleared by an even bigger lie. What's happened to Snotty Roddie, now?"

"I'm not sure, now that you're not going back to Valverde," Lenny mused. Then he smiled. "I wonder if Schuler has already expelled Roddie? He won't have to, now. You won't be back to make waves. What if he's already called Roddie's dad?"

"You're right, Lenny," I said. "Maybe I ought to call Schuler right now. He could..."

"I don't believe this," Lenny said. "It's one thing not to sue dear old VV, but aren't you going overboard? I mean, Schuler *is* a prime stiff, you know. And if Roddie comes back, Schuler can always hold this stunt over his head. Any way you look at it, Roddie's days as king of Valverde are over."

I smiled at Lenny. "Right, as usual, Mr. Rosenfeld," I said. "Tomorrow is time enough to call Schuler. But somehow, it gets to me. I'm trying hard not to carry a grudge, but dammit, Roddie may get away with it!"

"What do you care?" Lenny said. "You didn't want to go to VV to begin with. You weren't hurt by this. And Roddie may have learned a lesson. Unfortunately, I think the lesson is *don't get caught*."

"I don't like it," I said doggedly. "I wanted to be cleared, but not this way. It's just as phony as the way I was railroaded out of Valverde."

"Like it or not, you could at least give your faithful following a thank you for their efforts," said Lenny, somewhat miffed.

"Oh, of course, I thank you. Both of you," I replied. "I just..."

"You wanted the world to realize what a swell fellow you are and naturally clear you of any doubts. On your personal merits alone. Commendable, but impractical," Lenny said.

I could see that no matter how I phrased it, Lenny and even Natalie wouldn't understand what bothered me. So I just broke into a laugh I didn't really feel and said, "You're right. Both of you. I'm being foolish and acting like an ungrateful kid. Let's go have a swell dinner someplace!"

Which is just what we did. We all got into the two cars we had and took off for L.A. and Restaurant Row. I have to admit that Lenny sparkled all through dinner. We laughed long and hard, ate like Roman emperors, and even went dancing later. Or rather, Nat and I danced. Lenny watched, and tried to score with any chick that came within range of his magic line of B.S. But as good as he talks, Lenny has to clean up his act to get chicks. Or at least clear up his skin.

I drove Lenny back to VV with Nat following. It was too bad it worked out that way. I didn't get any time alone with Natalie until I walked her over to Brice House. At the door, I stopped. I couldn't bring myself to enter any building at Valverde. Not just then, anyhow.

"I want to thank you, Nat. Truly thank you," I told her. I put out my hand for a handshake. She grabbed me and kissed me. I guess I didn't respond the way I could have.

"What's wrong?" she asked.

"All this hasn't changed your mind about me... us, has it?" Her face fell. "No, Freddie, it hasn't," she admitted. "I have to do what I have to do. I owe it to my family."

"You're some piece of work, lady," I said. "You and Lenny, both. I love you, Nat. That's the trouble. And Lenny—he's hiding from life here at VV. He's somehow blamed his father for all he is, or isn't. And for all his protests about how he's an amused observer of life at Valverde, he's not that at all. He's scared to death of competing. Afraid he might fail. That's why he used me against Snotty Roddie. He coached me in how to dress. How to act. I learned a lot from Lenny."

"But he's your friend. A true friend!" Nat protested.

149

"I know he is," I answered. "That's why I˙say this to you and not to him. I believe a lot of what he says about Harry.

"Did you know that Harry had Lenny committed? It was after Lenny had that accident. He told me about that, and it's what keeps him at Valverde. If he quits, or gets out of line, he knows Harry will have him back in a rubber room in a flash.

"So he tries to get back at Harry by deliberately failing enough subjects not to graduate. But he shows enough brilliance to keep him on as a student. Harry's contributions to VV do the rest. He's got it in his mind that once he turns twenty-one, something magic will happen. He'll get rid of his rotten father and revenge his mother's death."

"Maybe you shouldn't be telling me this," Nat said. "I didn't know any of it. Just that Lenny's dad is Harry Rosenfeld of Galactic Pictures."

"I'm not telling you anything Lenny won't, first chance he gets. He's awful lonely, Nat. He wants desperately to tell someone. That's why he told me. But on the other hand, he's afraid someone will reject him. So he makes himself as unattractive as possible. He wants someone to see beyond the surface. To love him for himself."

"Are you sure you're not talking about Freddie Flores?" asked Natalie pointedly.

"Maybe I am," I conceded. "I was a misfit at Valverde, same as Lenny. That's what brought us together. The difference is, that I'm getting out.

Lenny could, too. If he could lie convincingly to Dean Schuler, he could lie his way out of VV by pretending he's changed his ways. Then, when he turned twenty-one, he could do as he pleased."

"He'd never do that," Nat reflected. "It wouldn't be winning. Not the way he wants to win."

"Ah-ha!" I said in triumph. "You can see that in Lenny, but you can't understand why I didn't feel great about winning out at Valverde."

"That's different, and you know it," Nat said.

"To you, maybe. Not to me," I replied. "And you can't see it. Same as you don't understand that you're hiding too, Nat."

"Me?"

"You bet. You say how much you care for me, but you cop out on the race thing. You say you owe it to your family. Maybe so. But you don't dedicate your life to some sort of goal you think your family wants for you. You have a commitment to only one person once the chips are down. I found that out when I lost my family.

"I realized how many things I did were in response to the wants of others. But now I realize that I have only one person I must be responsible to—me. Not the me that others see and judge. Not the me with *barrio* clothes on, or the me with Rodeo Drive clothes on. The me *inside* of me is who I have to please and live with.

"You want to give up someone you care for to please somebody else. Your family. That's why I

151

can't get too close to you, Nat. I did that before and got hurt."

"Freddie, it's more complicated than you paint it."

"To you. Listen, Nat. I have to go. Because if I stay here any longer, I'm going to lose my nerve. I'll probably take your company on your terms. That'd be fine for a while.

"Then that other me inside, the one I told you about, would start acting up. I can't do it. I love you, Nat. And if you should ever change your mind about things, you can always find me through Mrs. Fernandez. So long, Nat."

I turned and walked away. I had a small hope that she would call out to stop me. But she didn't. I guess she went straight into Brice House. I wouldn't know. I didn't look back....

I just read what I wrote down, only a year ago. I live in New York now. It made sense. I had gone over to thank Mr. Schwartzberg for his testimonial and for trying to help me. We had a long talk. He was happy that I was leaving Valverde. He told me that I'd make a terrible businessman, anyhow.

He also recommended me for the school I'm in now, the Art Student's League. I got in on my own merits, of course. And I'm doing well. Really well. I've learned more in the past six months about art and techniques than I could ever have done at VV.

What's more, I have friends here. They don't judge me by what I wear, just by my work and who I am. With each passing day, that me inside of me is getting closer to the me everyone sees. Nobody knows I have money. The great part is that none of my new friends seems to care, either.

I have a nice apartment in Greenwich Village. By Valverde standards, I suppose it's a rathole. But by Santa Amelia values, it's a good, clean place to live. It serves my needs. The greatest part of all is that I'm busy. I have a small studio I rented, near where I live. It's part of an artist's cooperative. We share expenses on the rent and facilities.

But that's not what made me look back at this story I wrote down when I first came to New York. What prompted me to look at it again was two letters I got in the mail today. One of them was from Mexico City, over a week old. It had gone to Callen's office first. He'd sent it, unopened, along with my regular weekly mail. I read it in disbelief. It was from a lawyer in Mexico City. My Aunt Tilda had died.

Dad was right. Aunt Tilda did have money. She left me a house in Mexico City and over a hundred thousand dollars. The letter said that she was being buried by a Catholic church society she belonged to. And I'd got the news too late to attend her funeral. I was secretly relieved. I don't think I could stand to bury another member of my family.

When I called Callen about the news, he had more to tell me. It seems that West Coastal Airlines is going to settle my claim within the next year. I now have more money than I'll ever be able to spend.

And for the life I've been leading, I don't even need it!

Then there was the second letter. It came from Natalie Simpson. She's decided that she wants to attend Sarah Lawrence College. That's just outside of New York City, in Westchester. She's coming to New York. And she'll be here for four years! Like she says in her letter:

> I've thought long and hard about the night you said goodbye, Freddie. You may be right. I'm not sure. I've acted on my feelings, though. I never wanted to be a lawyer. I've elected for a Fine Arts program at Sarah Lawrence. Yes, I know there are art schools just as fine out here. But they aren't close to you, in New York. That's why I'm coming out. I haven't broken with my family over this. You were right, though. They didn't get at all upset when I wanted to change my career goals. They just said if it made me happy, that was enough.
>
> And once I'm in New York, we can see more of each other, maybe...Oh, there's no point in maybes, is there? We'll find out once I'm there. We really didn't know each other all that well, Freddie. Just for about twelve weeks. I can say that I'm pretty sure already.
>
> Lenny sends his sardonic best. You were right about him. He told me all. Funny. He couldn't get Harry fired. Even with all that stock in the corporation. Harry has

done too good a job at Galactic over the years. It involved a proxy fight, and Lenny lost. I'm happy to say that it hasn't phased him. He's started up a company of his own, making music videos for TV. He seems to be on his way to making a fortune.

I'll be looking forward to September, Freddie. And you and New York.

Love, (I think)
Nat

I'm looking forward to September, too. Nat will be a stranger to New York. I can show her around. I wonder what she'll make of the Big Apple.

She'll probably get a kick out of nobody thinking I'm a Chicano. Everyone in New York sees me and they think I'm Puerto Rican. There are hardly any Mexicans in New York.

The Puerto Ricans don't think I'm Puerto Rican, though. They get a big kick out of my Chicano accent. And I get one word in five of what they say in Spanish. They talk so fast!

But no matter what happens, it won't throw me. So long as I stay within the bounds of what Lenny calls my "curious integrity."

It's been a long day, and I'm about to sack out. I wonder how Mrs. Fernandez is getting on in her new house, my old one? Probably watching "Happy Days." Me too, but without a TV set.